Sam's L

Patricia McGuinness

ISBN: 978-1-326-82180-7

PublishNation
www.publishnation.co.uk

Remembering my husband, Tony, who didn't live to see this finished.

My thanks to friends and family for their support and encouragement.

Chapter 1

Once she had left the M5 and joined the A5, the journey improved, although the weather was a resolute drab drizzle. On and on she drove and the atmosphere just seemed to echo the way she felt, grey and desolate. With Shrewsbury far behind her, she soon began to see signs in both English and Welsh, and realised that, for the first time in her life, she was in Wales. She had already decided to stop the night before dark, and on a day of such gloom, dark was going to fall early, so she began to look out for a hotel or a B&B. On the outskirts of a small town, she found a roadside public house with a B&B sign, and she drove down the side into a small car park, stopped the car close to the doors, pulled on the handbrake and turned off her lights and wipers. She didn't want to be caught out with a flat battery come morning. She loved her little Fiesta, but it was far from new and needed to be coddled a bit. If only somebody would coddle her. She sat for a couple of minutes, just winding down from her long drive, before she shook herself, picked up her leather holdall, Sam's holdall from the passenger seat and stepped out into the rain and the chill of late afternoon in early November in mid-Wales.

"Yes." There was a room available, in fact she was the first person to book in on this Tuesday afternoon, as the young girl with long coppery hair had told her.

"We usually get a couple of reps, but that's about it at this time of year," she said as Ella gave her details. "The makings are in your room, No. 3, but, if you like I can fetch you a pot of tea in the lounge bar by the fire."

The mention of a fire settled it and she took her room key and went through the swing door into a room with a busy pub carpet and some comfortable, old-fashioned looking chairs. In a wide stone fireplace was a cheerful log fire and Ella put down her bags and settled into a chair close to the comfort of the flames. It was a large chair and t seemed to swallow her up, so that she had to pull herself more upright before the girl came in with a tray, which she placed on a small, brass-topped table. On the tray was an EPNS teapot, jug and basin and a cup and saucer and plate with a border of ivy leaves. On the plate were three or four custard creams. The girl, who said her name was Jenny, smiled at her and then went back to the reception area. It was such a simple, welcoming gesture that Ella could have cried. Not that that was difficult. She was bone weary and drained. She heard sweet tea helped and, after a while she relaxed a little and began to study the room. It was a little shabby, but pleasing at the same time. The wainscoting was a deep sage green and the walls above a rich cream and there were striped green and cream curtains on the three large windows, which Jenny drew before she collected her tray.

"Breakfast is 7:30 'till 8:30 she told Ella. "I expect you will want a proper breakfast in this miserable weather."

Ella hesitated – food had no interest for her anymore – but she had to be sensible.

"Would it be possible to have scrambled eggs on toast?" she asked.

"Yes, of course. What about tonight? We do bar snacks, sandwiches and such."

"Perhaps a tuna sandwich."

"Righty-ho. Your room is the second on the left up by the stairs," and she took the tray and left.

There was a lot of framed photos on the walls in dark frames and nicely grouped. Ella noticed such things. She dragged herself out of the chair and went to inspect them, almost surprising herself. They were all from about the 1920's or so, with a few older ones also. Most of them were of cows and sheep, men and carts and some were of a cattle market. 'Welshpool Cattle Market' she read on one and realized that it was the next place she had been heading for. Obviously its market had been a major part of it in the '20's.

Chapter 2

Before she went upstairs, she pushed a door which opened into the bar. There were a couple of men there, probably having a pint on the way home from work. Behind the bar was a small, round man with thin copper-coloured hair. He looked over as she approached and then smiled. She asked for a tuna sandwich and he wrote it on a pad and pushed the slip through a hatch.

"Filthy night," he said, and she agreed.

"Come far?"

"Yes, quite a long drive."

"Going far?"

"Yes, quite far."

Obviously realizing he wasn't going to get much in the way of a conversation, he turned away, only to return when her sandwich appeared at the hatch.

"You needn't pay now," he said, as she began to fish for her wallet. "I'll put it on your bill for the morning."

She thanked him and said, "Good night," and as she made her way upstairs, she thought, *He must be the landlord. I wonder if he's the girl's father?* She noticed they had the same hair colour.

It was a heavy old door to the room and she began to see that this was really quite an old building. She hadn't looked at the outside and suddenly realized that she didn't even know the name of the place, or the pub. Oh well. What did it matter?

The room was dated but comfortable. The furniture was solid and dark, but the wallpaper was buttercup yellow, with small sprigs of flowers and the curtains were in matching fabric. She dumped her holdalls and dragged the curtains across. She could now hear the rain, so she knew it must have become heavier.

There was a small padded chair and a TV on top of the chest. She idly switched it on – it was nearly news time – and had a look in the bathroom. It was old-fashioned, but clean, serviceable and a very decent supply of towels. Turning her attention to the bed she discovered a very traditional eiderdown, with two blankets and decent, squashy pillows. She pushed off her brogues and wondered about a bath, but decided she really couldn't be bothered.

A shower would do in the morning. Putting the 'DO NOT DISTURB' sign on the outside doorknob, she fished her pyjamas out and changed into them. She loved her jimjams and would have liked to live in them, really. Sam used to call her Jimjam Ella.

No! Don't think of Sam!

As a diversion, she sat down and began to eat her sandwich.

The news was as depressing as the weather. Young soldiers dying in Iraq, the world's financial crisis, cheating MPs. She turned it off in disgust and looked about her for reading material. There was the usual Bible – no thank you – and a couple of decent country magazines and a list of guest information on The Woolpack, Welshpool. That was where she was, and sure enough, it dated from 1810. It was at a crossroads with an old road that had been a drovers' track, from when the local sheep had been brought to market by a man and his dog. Obviously they used pick-ups now, she reasoned, but she knew nothing at all about sheep. It seemed, from a potted local history, that the market at Welshpool had been one of the biggest livestock markets in Wales. Her route tomorrow took her through Welshpool, along the A548 before she turned northwards. She'd left her map book in the car, as it would be time enough to consider her next stage in the morning. Suddenly, she felt weary. It was only 7:30, but did it matter? She longed to sleep her life away anyway, and she needed to be up early. She took her pill with a glass of water and climbed into the high old bed, tuned off the lamp and snuggled down. Just before she drifted off she had a mental image of dozens of dozens of sheep trailing around the corner of the pub's old walls.

Chapter 3

When she did wake up, it was still dark and she lay there for a while. The tablets her doctor in Bath had prescribed certainly made her sleep, but she had to drag herself awake from them. With a start, she realised her watch read 7:30, the longest she'd slept for in a while. She found a shower cap in a little bag in the bathroom and turned on the shower. She didn't have the time to get her hair wet, as it took ages to dry, although it was really thick and had a natural curl and needed to be tamed after it was washed. She dragged it back into its usual ponytail and pulled on her jeans and thick pale blue sweater. After a quick swipe of lipstick and with her bags packed and ready to roll, she went down for some coffee and eggs.

Sure enough, just as Jenny had said, there were two lone men, eating a full English, or as she supposed, a full Welsh. It was strange to be in a different country, but Jenny only had the slightest of Welsh lilts to her voice.

"Are you off anywhere exciting?" she asked now, as she served her eggs.

"I don't know," replied Ella. "I won't know until I get there." and she left it at that.

When she paid her bill in cash she gave Jenny a couple of pounds and thanked her for her welcome.

"That's what we're here for," she laughed. "Anytime you're passing – safe journey."

If anything, the weather was worse than before and a very frisky wind was blowing. She ran out to her car and slammed her door against the wind. The bags went in the back and she picked up her map book, at the same time as turning the ignition and pressing the de-mist button. She knew this old car. The book was open on pages 60-61 and there was Welshpool. As she traced the route she saw the next place to look out was Mallwyd and it dawned on her that she really was entering Welsh Wales. The place names became stranger and stranger and what was with all the 'y's and double 's's

Sychtyn – how on earth would you pronounce that? she thought.

Also, further ahead on her route became pale green and that signified Snowdonia National Park. Of course she had heard about Snowdon – everyone had, so she knew she was going to see some mountains. Apart from a wonderful trip with Sam to Andorra, she was not very familiar with mountains. Around Bath and Bristol were only rolling hills and her childhood home in the Midlands hadn't even got those. She checked her petrol gauge and decided to fill up as soon as she could. She'd only just pulled out onto the road when she saw a 'Welcome to Welshpool' sign, followed by a Shell garage. She bought a big bar of Fruit and Nut and put it on the passenger seat, out of reach of her meagre hot air jet. Then, on a sudden whim, she ran back in and grabbed a bottle of Lucozade.

Right, she thought, *I'm ready*.

The road did take her on a one-way circuit through the town and, in spite of the rain, she spotted attractive old black and white houses and a brief glimpse of the Cattle Market, still busy obviously. Then she was out on the open road and beginning to climb slowly.

Bearing north and Mallwyd and onwards to Minllyn she went, marvelling at the strange names. She crossed a big bridge and guessed there might be views on a better day and before too long, she reached Dolgellau. She pulled over and had a few cubes of chocolate and a swig from her drink and and set off again. In spite of herself she began to feel a flicker of interest, This was very new to her and she could not believe the sheep, who were thick in every field, mostly in a huddle against dry stone walls, sheltering from the day. Whilst driving on a long straight stretch and she thought, *I know a Welsh word* as it dawned on her that *afon* must mean river. The rain was easing slightly, but it had left behind a thick, swirling mist through which she sited a huge lake n her left. After that, the road twisted and turned and she had to keep her wits about her. She knew she must be going through the mountains and the road dipped and rose quite a lot, but visibility was awful and she was concentrating hard, so that it came as a surprise to her when she suddenly found herself running down a long hill to arrive at the start of a sort of causeway. To her left was a very high wall and an old toll both, and she could just make out water and cows (was she imagining the cows?) on the far right. It was narrow and there were a couple of lorries and a bus approaching, and she was glad to find herself at the end of it and running into Porthmadog. There was a station and lots of shops and restaurants and it seemed to be a thriving place, even in this weather.

It was lunchtime, but she wasn't hungry and she'd nibbled chocolate all morning, so she drove through, realizing soon after she should have looked for a toilet sign, but she was soon in Criccieth, where she did stop. She was on sea level and there were the ruins of a castle and interesting shops and she found a sweet little cafe, where she had hot chocolate, her favourite hot drink. Getting close now, with a short run to Pwllheli (yes) and then just seven or eight miles to Abersoch. The narrow road was quiet now and Ella caught the occasional glimpse of the flat, steel grey sea across the fields. She stopped in a lay-by and re-read the agent's details. She had to turn right at the first turning, by a big boat chandlers, as she dropped into the village, which she did. The about ¼ mile passing a few white painted cottages and bungalows and a gap before she saw, on her right, a 'For Sale' sign. She checked the time – half an hour to kill, so she finished her snack and settled down to listen to the car radio. All she could see across the lane was a low green hedge just showing above a dry stone wall and a slate roof, with two dormer windows set in. *What am I doing here?* was her last thought before she dozed off.

Chapter 4

She woke with a start to a tapping sound.   In the gloom outside was a young woman in a Barbour jacket, tapping gently on her window. Embarrassed, she turned off the radio, ran her fingers through her hair and opened the door.   The girl from the estate agents stood back and held her hand out and smiled.

"Sorry to startle you." she said, as they shook hands.   "I'm Gaynor Ackersley, and you must be Miss Hodson."

"Do call me Ella, I'm so sorry I was asleep.   It's been a long drive."

"Where have you driven from?"

"I've come from Welshpool today and left Bath yesterday."

"Oh, it's a long trail even when the weather is good," and she stepped across the lane and opened a blue wooden gate set in the wall.

They stepped into a wide flat expanse of grass neatly cut and bisected by a slate path.

"Be careful," Gaynor said.   "These slates are lethal in the wet." As she spoke, she pulled a bunch of keys out of her pocket and chose a big one to put in the lock of the door.   This door was set right in the middle, with a low bay window on either side.   Above these windows were the dormers she had seen from the car.   Ella turned to look at the view, but there was only grey mist and drizzle.   The stepped on through the solid old door into quite a large room and hastily shut the door.   To the left was a doorway and on the far wall a wooden staircase ran across the space, with a smaller window set almost in the corner.   It was empty and the big stone hearth held only ashes.   Chill as it was and bare of any colour, it wasn't unwelcoming.   The fireplace wall was stone and the other three walls were white.   The windowsills were deep and there were old-fashioned wall-lights placed around.   Ella notice that the ceilings were a decent height and commented on it to Gaynor, who stood quietly, letting her study the room.

"Yes," she said, "the ceilings are good, and you need them to be, at your height. As for me, I fit anywhere." and they both smiled.

Gaynor could not have looked any less like Ella. She was probably about 5 ft tall and, even in her Barbour, you could see she was curvy. Her hair was cut in an elfin style and very dark and she had round rosy cheeks and laughing eyes.

After a moment or two, she stepped across to open the other door in the room. Ella was surprised when she entered, because she had assumed it would be a kitchen. Instead, it was a room similar to the other. It also had a large stone fireplace and the same bay, but it didn't stretch as far back. In the back wall was another door, the same stone wall and white paint and Ella realized that the cottage was larger than she had thought. Through the other door must be the kitchen – and it was. It ran across the width of the house and was plain and functional. There was a Belfast sink and a few yellow-fronted Formica units, an elderly cooker and that was it. The floor was stone-flagged and Ella realised she hadn't looked at the other floors. She stood back to look through the door and saw plain dark grey carpet. At the left side of the kitchen, there was an archway, which led into a small area plumbed for a washer and at the opposite end a half-glazed door. The window was above the sink area. It was quite roomy, larger than she would have thought.

Gaynor picked up on her thoughts and said, "It's quite large, isn't it? You could really make something of it, but obviously, it would need money spending on it. There's no central heating, as you know, and the water heats from the main fire and an immersion heater. The couple who lived here had been here forever. She died some few years ago, and he stayed on here, on his own, until about three years ago he went into care in Pwllheli and died in February. He seems to have had just the one relative, a man living in Cheshire and he's decided to sell up."

She smiled. "I'm not going to do what we call at the office a 'Kirsty' on you, but I can see a lot of potential here. Let's show you upstairs."

The stairs led up to a small landing, with an equally small window and three doors. The bathroom proved to be of the same era as the kitchen and pretty basic. One of the bedrooms had enough room, they thought, for twin beds and Gaynor ran her measure over it to be certain. There were good, deep cupboards in both the alcoves, one fitted out with shelving and the dormer window. It seemed very dark. Then again, as the agent said, it was mid-afternoon on a filthy November day! Because of that, the other bedroom surprised her. It seemed so much larger and lighter. There was another window in the corner alcove, like the one downstairs and she stood trying to work out which way she was looking.

"That one looks right across the harbour beach and across to Harlech," a voice said at her shoulder. "That view must be the reason why they built this place with those two extra windows. The dormers are too high for me, but you should be able to look out from them." and she could, although all she saw was swirling rain and mist.

"Can I have just a little wander around?"

"Of course. I'll wait downstairs, no hurry."

Ella paced about upstairs. The hot water tank was in a cupboard in the bathroom, complete with shelving. For some strange reason Ella began to feel more peaceful than she had for months. The house seemed to be saying, "It's safe here, just relax."

She ran down the stairs and said to Gaynor, "Can I come back when I've slept on it?"

"Sure you can, but don't hang about too long. This place is a honeypot for second home owners and cottages like this don't take long to sell. Actually, this time of year is a bit slower, but even so," she said. "Where are you staying? I'll give you my card with my mobile number on and you can get in touch directly. I do live in the village – well, the edge of the village and I could be around and about in the morning."

"I don't actually know where I'm staying. I'm only here for one night, as I have left a dog with a friend. Any suggestions?"

"Try the Riverside Hotel. It's over the bridge and just on the corner. It's quite small, but it does stay open through winter when some of them don't. And it has a good Chinese eat-in or takeaway. Just turn right at the bottom of the hill."

They shook hands on it when suddenly Ella said, "Oh, can we just look around outside?" and they locked the door and walked along the side of the house. There seemed to be quite an expanse of grass and a few small trees in the background. To one side there was a stone outhouse, which looked in decent condition.

"Right, thanks for that. I'll give you a call in the morning."

They both turned their cars in a big gateway and followed each other down the hill, where Gaynor turned left. The hotel was nearby and she pulled in just over the bridge. There was a wide stream running across the end of the car park and a lot of lawn. Everywhere was very quiet. She got her map book and bag and pulled the hood of her jacket over her head and went to find a way in. The reception area was a large table, with a bowl of fresh flowers and a hand bell. 'Please ring if you need us' read the handwritten card, so she did. There was the sound of clumping footsteps coming upwards on the open-tread spiral staircase, then a bald, tanned plate appeared, atop a smiling tanned face followed by a well-fed shape.

"Good day, madam." the man smiled as he spoke and Ella immediately thought, *I like him.* "Can I help?"

"I hope so, I want a single room, just for tonight, please?"

"Madam," he said, "you can have the best room in the place, basic price, as you will be our only guest. At best, that how it looks so far. Just sign here for me and I'll take your bags. Your room is on the side overlooking the river, it's a quiet room you should sleep well."

He threw open the door onto a big room almost filled with a pine four-poster bed. Having placed her bags on a small chest he swept the curtains closed and showed her the makings for a drink and the controls for the TV.

"Would you want to eat in?" he asked.

"Could I just have something simple," Ella inquired. "as I'm not very hungry."

"Certainly, you can. How about my special crab and sweetcorn chowder? The crab was still asleep on the bay last night." he grinned.

"That sounds good. OK if I come down about 7?"

"Perfect." he said. "I'll have a fire lit in the bar. I only open the restaurant at weekends at this time of the year. Mind you, I do plenty of takeaways in the week and then I enjoy the buzz at the weekend."

He shut the door behind him and she threw herself onto the huge bed. Time to consider.

Chapter 5

The fire was lit and there was soft lighting from the table lamps in the bar and the chowder, when it arrived, was more than delicious. It was served with a couple of chunks of warm bread and Ella polished it off with the first real hunger she had felt in an age.

"My name is Tudor." the man said when he came for the empty plates. "Tudor Evans. During off-peak I'm a bit of a one-man band on week nights. I have a cleaner in the morning, but I run the bar and do the cooking."

"Your soup was really great. I've not enjoyed anything so much in ages."

"If you're still peckish, I have some great local cheeses."

"Do you know, I think I could eat some more. Yes, please."

When he came back, he had a slate board with three cheeses on it. One was a blue-veined Llyn, another a goat's cheese from two miles away and the other from Plas Nefyn – a strong, tasty one. There were oatcakes and a dash of salty butter and he placed it all on the table and returned with a glass in his hand.

"Try that," he said, "on me."

That turned out to be a rich ruby port, which went down so well that she began to relax and enjoy herself.

Tudor stayed behind the bar, but chatted, and she found she wanted to chat to this pleasant man.

"What are you doing all the way out here, then? Abersoch doesn't see many strangers in winter."

She found herself confiding in this man that she had been to look at a cottage and was seriously considering moving here.

"Are you on your own?" he asked.

"Well, apart form a dog, yes I am."

"Have you been on the Llyn before?"

"Never. Never even been in Wales, but I need to move on."

"Do you have work lined up? There are lots of jobs from Easter onwards, but it isn't so easy right now."

"I don't need to work immediately, but anyway I have to get a feel for the place, in the morning, before I decide."

"Yes," he said, "you do that. Have a good rest and then explore in the morning. How would local sausage and fried eggs do?"

"Perfect. I have enjoyed this evening. Thank you, Tudor." and she wandered off to her bed with her thoughts.

She slept well and woke early. Climbing out of her huge bed she pulled back the curtains. Somehow she had assumed it would be grey and wet, but it was another world entirely. She was looking out at blue clear sky and a view out over the bridge of blue, green and white flecked sea and white cottages; boats and distant mountains. Her heart lifted. She was down early and Tudor was pottering.

"Why don't you have a little look at the place before you eat?" he suggested, so she ran to grab her jacket and watched the ducks bobbing about on the river as she shrugged into it. Across the bridge there were wooden seats and she had a brief perch to take it all in. Under her feet the river ran out towards the beach and eventually met the sea. There were boatyards and a lifeboat station and she thought of St Ives, where she and Sam had spent their last   little holiday together. On she went into Abersoch. There were quite a lot of small shops, with clothes and surfing gear, food and all sorts of other things. They were all still shut. Ella was surprised at the variety of cafes and bars. It all looked clean and looked after. There was nothing tacky. She saw at least two places selling local craft goods and she really liked what she saw. A little lane led down to the river and the end cottage stood almost in the water. Ella could see that the tide came in a long way and decided she would love to see it with the tide in – but how? Then it really struck her. All she needed to do was make an offer on the cottage and she could see the high tide whenever she wanted. Immediately she was impatient to see it again. She looked at her watch (well, Sam's watch). It was almost 8 o'clock. By the time she had breakfast it should be OK to call Gaynor.

She called in on Gaynor, in her offices and asked for the names of reputable local workmen and spent another night at the Riverside. Then, with a last stroll about the village she was ready for off.

She had discovered a group of buildings, on the road up to the cottage, which housed hand carved, individual, artist enterprises, including a carpenter, a photographer and her imagination had begun to go into overdrive, but *Hang on, let's get it all sorted first*, she thought.

Chapter 6

Corby was not the most exciting place in which to grow up and 29 Mather Close was not the sort of home you missed greatly. Ella lived there with her Ma and Pa and Grandpa, at least, that was before Grandpa died. It was a council house, neat and terraced. Her Ma called it a quasi-semi, but nobody else did. Ma was like that. She always thought she was too good to be living there and had few friends. Ella knew the neighbours thought she was stuck-up, although they were all friendly enough with her and Da. Grandpa came to live with them when his wife died and Ella was about four years old. He was Pa's father and he had the small bedroom. She loved her Grandpa, as she loved her Pa. They were very similar to look at, both burly men with beards. Pa's was light and Grandpa's was white and they both had fair skin with freckles. Pa used to let her learn to count on his freckles, but she never got them all. They both laughed a lot and had fun with the little girl.

Ma was different. Ella took after her in her looks, people always said, with her flaxen hair and deep brown eyes. She was slightly built too like Annunciate and moved like her, but she did hope she didn't have such a cross-looking face. Very little seemed to please her and she ignored any merriment caused by the men. She went to Mass at the local church every Friday and took Ella with her on Sundays. Her only social outing was to a Women's Guild on Monday evenings and, just very occasionally, to the cinema with Pa. The house always felt more relaxed when she was out and Grandpa or Pa were in charge.

Ella did realize, as she grew older, that her Ma did a good job. The house was neat as a pin and they were fed well. Annie, as her pa called her Ma, made most of Ella's clothes and they were always mended and ironed nicely. It was just that there was always a feeling of disapproval about Annie.

Grandpa grew vegetables on a strip of the small back garden and the young child helped him. She loved picking tiny carrots and peas that grew up the fence. When they picked peas they used to sit on the rusty seat with a bowl between them and a pail on the ground. They pressed the green pods and they popped open, which fascinated Ella. The big fat peas went in the bowl and the tiny underdeveloped ones into their mouths. The pods went in the pail and onto the compost heap.

One summer afternoon, sitting there with her grandfather, Ella saw him grasp at his chest.

"Get your Ma, Ella." he gasped.

Then it all became a flurry and they took Grandpa away in an ambulance with a bell ringing.

"What's happened to Grandpa?" she tearfully asked.

"We have to wait and see and pray," answered her Ma.

But the prayers didn't work and the next morning, Da told her that her Granddad had died and gone the Heaven. She was four when it happened and it was the first horrid thing to happen to her. She missed him and the home was very quiet while Da was at wok.

He worked as a bricklayer and once said he had no alternative, as he was known all over as 'Rod the Hod', but she thought he was kidding her. Ma called him Roderick, his pals 'Rod the Hod and other people, 'Mr Hodson'. He told Ella his name was a Viking one, from the invaders of the east coast hundreds of years ago, and she liked that idea. It made her family seem more exciting.

Soon after Grandpa's death, she began school and soon made a best friend, Nancy, who lived on the same estate. Nancy came from a family of six children and she was in the middle. Ella was much quicker at her lessons, but it didn't matter to them and their friendship grew stronger. Neither of them liked to stand out in a crowd and played together most of the time – ball games and hopscotch. On light evenings, they were allowed out for an hour after tea and Ma taught them how to knit on big fat needles. They both made long scarves for their dolls and then stripy ones for themselves and were very pleased with their handiwork. They assumed they would always be together. On some Saturdays Da would go fishing and the two girls went with him, to a reservoir not too far away. While Da fished they entertained themselves collecting pebbles and wildflowers. They became experts at pebble throwing to bounce across the still waters. They had cheese butties and bananas and orange squash and Da always had a 'warmer' in a little flask.

But Ella discovered that another good thing was to come to an end. Inevitably, she got a scholarship place at a local convent high school while Nancy went to a big, rough secondary modern. Their schools were in different directions and they needed to go by bus to get there. Ella began to get a lot of homework and they had very little time to play out. It was time for her tea when she got home and she just had a few minutes to get out of her red and grey uniform before she and her parents sat down to eat. It was always a hot meal, pie and mash or corned beef has. Ma had a set pattern of meals, so you knew what toe expect, and it was always fish on Fridays. Ella did her homework. Da had put a desk in the room his dad had used and Ella had a shelf for her growing collection of books, because she loved to read. With her small amount of pocket money she would have a root in charity shops and buy all sorts of books that took her fancy. She picked up one about Normandy and its history and links with Britain and there was a lot of information about the Bayeux Tapestry and coloured sketches of it. *Fancy being able to embroider history*, thought the twelve-year-old Ella. She loved English, Art and History lessons the best and wasn't very good at Games. With her long legs she could run fast and jump far, but she wasn't very co-ordinated or into team games, so she just did what she needed to do to keep out of trouble.

School wasn't too bad, really. Some of the nuns were really great teachers, who had all the time in the world to explain the more difficult ideas and the art mistress picked up on a talent in Ella and encouraged her. Sometimes, after Mass on Sunday, she and Nancy would be allowed a coffee together in a little coffee shop near the church. Nancy wasn't very happy at school and Ella found herself holding back from telling her some of her more interesting nuns. The art class were being taken on a day trip to a local stately home and she was really looking forward to it. It was on a Monday and there were about thirty of them, all in their smart uniforms and with lunch in their bags. Just being together on a bus was fun and Ella was really fascinated by the beauty of the objects they saw. What thrilled her most of all was the tapestries and the glorious colours used on the house walls. Deep crimsons and dark greys, duck egg blue and sunny yellow. She was used to cream at home. She made notes and did little sketches and enjoyed it all so very much.

So she was still on a high when she got home. She knew there was something wrong as soon as she saw Ma. She had been crying – a thing almost unheard of.

"Sit down, Ella," she said. "I have some bad news – no, no, it's not your Da, he's still at work. I'm afraid, love, it's Nancy."

Nancy, how could it be Nancy? She was only fourteen, like Ella.

"She was on the back of her brother's bike when they went into a tree. She flew off over his head and she's," at this point she dragged a soggy hankie out from her apron and wept, "she's – I'm sorry, Ella, she died there and then."

Ella sat stock still while she took in her mother's words. Then she jumped to her feet and ran upstairs and threw herself on her bed. She lay crying and then sobbing for a long time. Her Ma brought her a cup of tea and patted her on the head and then left. Some time later, she heard her Da's voice and then he was in her room.

"Eh, lass," he said, "Come here." and he threw his arms around her and held her while she sobbed.

The funeral was very sad. Nancy's father and uncles and older brother carried her white coffin and there were many tearful teenagers. They were all in a state of shock. Everyone tried to avoid catching the eye of Billy, the brother who had crashed and who had aged twenty years in a week.

For weeks, an awful pall hung over them all, but they were only young and gradually things returned to normal, but Ella had lost her first friend, after her Grandpa.

Life at home was becoming grimmer. Ella heard her parents rowing and Da spent more time at the pub and playing his ukulele with like-minded folks. Ella was being encouraged to go on to Uni, and, for once, Ma approved. Ella worked hard and ignored the atmosphere at home and did really well with her A-levels.

Chapter 7

She had applied to do History of Art at Bristol and Ma and Da drove her there, in the van, to see what it was all about. The uni buildings were mostly in the centre of the town and Ella would be allocated in nearby halls. She thought it all looked wonderful. Bristol itself looked interesting and the countryside was much softer and prettier. They had a tourist view of the Suspension Bridge and the old quays, now trendy bars and bistros. She felt she would enjoy living there.

To the delight of all of them she got her place. The summer she was eighteen passed in a flurry of getting ready to leave home. She had to provide certain things for her room, and, of course, she wanted to take her books. Ma made her some new shirts and bought her jeans and jerseys and, eventually, the day came. The three of them made the cross-country trip again and waited while all the formalities took place and then settled her in her new home.

It was a reasonable-sized room, with a bed, a desk and chair and an easy chair, there were lots of shelves and Ella noticed small scars on the wall, where posters had been. She was to share both kitchen and bathroom with three other female students, one of them she met as they looked round.

"Hello, I'm Jackie Moor," she said as she shook hands.

"And I'm Ella Hodson."

"Where are- ?"

"What are - ?"

an embarrassing pause followed and then Ella said, "Where are you from?"

"Hereford, right in the middle, really and I'm here to do Geology, what about you?"

"I'm taking History of Arts and I'm from Corby."

They grinned at each other and then they and their parents drifted off to unpack. After they had settled her in and put some dishes and pans in the kitchen, her mother said, "Well, let's go shopping for some food to start you off and then something to eat."

And off they went. They discovered a Tesco Express very close by, so they went first to a pizza place. Ella's stomach churned with a mixture of apprehension and excitement and it took all her time to get through a good half of her Margarita.

"Here, lass, push it over," Roderick said, and immediately came a sharp retort from Annie.

"I do believe, Roderick, that you'd eat at your own funeral."

He grinned sheepishly, and Ella thought, not for the first time, *Leave it alone, Ma, he's alright.*

Quick farewells taken , off they went and Ella drifted into the shared kitchen and began putting away the basic food stuff Ma had bought. Da had pushed £60 into her hand and given her a long hug. It all felt very strange. After a few minutes, Jackie appeared in the doorway. She was red-eyed and had obviously been crying.

"Fancy a coffee?" asked Ella and, when Jackie nodded she filled the communal kettle and plugged it in. Then she got two of her six mugs out and spooned coffee from her new jar of Nescafe.

"Milk and sugar, please," said Jackie, as she came across to perch on a stool.

"It's all a bit weird, isn't it?"

"Yes, but very exciting. Have you ever lived away before? I haven't but I'm looking forward to it."

"I will miss my little brother. He's only five and he's just begun in Reception and he comes home full of it. I've got a brother of thirteen, but he's just a pain in the arse."

They sat chatting about families and home towns until they heard more people arriving in the hallway and, after a short while, two other families crowded into the kitchen. They all spoke to introduce themselves. Myra and Joanne were the new arrivals and they were so similar in looks that it was difficult not to stare. They had mid-brown bobbed hair and very rosy cheeks and were about 5'3" or 4". The only big difference was in their accent, and it turned out that one came from Penrith and one from Brighton, so that was understandable.

Eventually the families had all gone and the four girls were left to sort themselves out and make decisions about sharing the fridge etc.

Jackie seemed the most confident, with a strong sense of humour and a ready laugh.   She declared that Myra and Joanne were so similar that they were probably long-lost twins, mysteriously separated at birth and declared she was going to call them, 'Twin One' and 'Twin Two' and, over mugs of hot chocolate and much hilarity that is what they became.

For an only child, like Ella, from such an old-fashioned home this was all a revelation and she felt a great surge of anticipation at what life was going to be like here in Bristol.

Chapter 8

They all survived Freshers' Week, nursing the odd hangover and settled in very amicably together. Twin One – Myra – was on the same degree course as Ella, so they were able to help each other and compare notes.

They had a communal telephone in the main hallway and Ella rang home once a week. She had stilted conversations with her Ma and very rarely seemed to catch her Da in, which she was sad about, as he was always so much more loving with her, but she was not in the least bit feeling homesick. Life was too much fun.

One evening a boy from another flat answered the phone, which was ringing when he passed it. "Is there an Ella in there?" he shouted. "Ella Hodson!" and she ran out to the phone.

It was Ma. "I've some bad news for you, Ella. It's about your father."

Ella's heart skipped a beat.

"OK, Ma, what's happened?" she gabbled into the phone. "Is he dead?"

"Oh, no child, nothing like that, but he's gone. He's left a note and he's gone."

"Gone, what do you mean, Ma, gone?"

"He's left us, Ella. He said he'll send me the money for the rent every month and let you have what he can manage. I'll have to find a job."

"Do you know where he is? Have you got an address?"

"Nothing, not a thing – selfish to the core, your father."

Even battling with her shock, Ella thought, *No, he's not. You've pushed him away,* but what she said was some sympathetic noises.

"Take care, Ma, I'll ring in a day or two." and she put the receiver down and walked, shakily, back to her room.

"OK, Da, what have you done?"

Two days later she got a letter and recognised the ill-formed hand

– it was from Da. He told her he had managed to keep sane while he had her company to enjoy, but now she had flown the nest he couldn't bear to spend the rest of his life trapped with Annie. "She saps the very life out of me," he wrote, and Ella knew he told the truth. He enclosed two £20 notes and told her how proud he was of her and how he would always love her dearly. He would keep in touch, but there was no forwarding address. She wept onto the scrawled page. She would miss him so much, but in her heart, he had done what was right for him.

Her three companions were sympathetic and talked her through. Joanne, Twin Two, lived with her widowed mother, at least Ella still had a Da. Life fell into its small routines and they were all busy.

Jackie went off on a field study into South Wales and came home talking about this incredible tutor. Gradually she talked of little else and they became curious about this bloke. He never came near halls and Jackie only saw him maybe once every couple of weeks, so Myra did a bit of nosing around. She discovered he was in his mid 30s and married with either one or two young children.

"Did Jackie know?!" they asked themselves, and should they tell her or not.

In the end, they decided to just try and ignore it and this they did until they all split up for Christmas. Ella was dreading going to her cheerless home and Myra asked her if she would fancy spending New Year at her home in Penrith. "You can have Christmas with your Mum," she said, "and catch a train up to Penrith and Mike could meet you."

At least that would be something to look forward to. To forewarn her mother and in the hopes of not ruining Christmas, she wrote and explained her plans before they finished the term.

She bought her mother a fine coral pink pashmina and wrapped it carefully. There was no van and no Da, so Corby had to be reached by bus and then train and it was not something to be excited about.

When she got home, it was to the usual cool greeting. Ma had got herself a job as a receptionist for a local dentist and was just about coping. Da sent the rent and a bit more, but she was very bitter. Ella climbed in the loft and dragged down the little artificial tree and the box of lights and did her best to cheer the place up.

She walked round one evening to visit Nancy's family and the difference was so marked she could have wept. The house buzzed with young people and there were streamers and bunches of mistletoe. Billy looked much better than when she had last seen him and grabbed her under the mistletoe. The both laughed and he said it was good to see her again. Would she go out with a gang of them on Friday for a Christmas drink? She arranged to be ready at 7:30 and Billy said he'd call for her and they could walk to the pub together.

Ma, of course, was disapproving, but Ella stood her ground and was glad she did. She knew most of the crowd and they all seemed happy to include her. There were lots of questions about what she was doing and about Bristol. She only felt a bit of coolness from one girl, who obviously had a bit of a thing for Billy.

Ella smiled to herself. Billy was just Nancy's brother and there was no suggestion that they fancied each other. In fact, when she considered the thought, there wasn't anybody she felt that way about at all. There was time enough for that. Nancy's older sister, Pam, had just got engaged, which shocked Ella. She must have been nineteen and he was a lovely lad who looked about 16. Anyway, they raised a toast to them and, later, they all went on to another pub, singing carols en route. It was a fun night, but Ella's spirits slumped when she got home. Ma asked her nothing about the evening and only said, "I hope you've not drunk too much, my lady."

In the morning, Christmas Eve, there were two cards from Da. Annie opened hers in the kitchen and Ella saw her put some money in her purse, on the dresser. The card wasn't mentioned and didn't appear. Her Da had put £40 in hers and lots of love to her for a Happy Christmas. Later, when her Ma was upstairs Ella rooted in the bin and found her Da's crumpled card. He wished Annie a peaceful Christmas and, briefly, told her his news. He was working again and was in old-fashioned digs and should be able to send her a little more cash every month. Her Da had always dealt in cash, although he and Ma had a Post Office account. Well, at least Ella knew he was safe, although, back in such familiar surroundings her heart ached to see him and hear his cheery voice.

They went together to Midnight Mass and one of the ladies from church invited them for some lunch on the 27th. Christmas Day was grim and the TV was on most of the time because they had very little to say to each other. They'd never had really and now it was worse; a glass of sherry and a ham salad lunch was the highlight of those festive days. Ella realised that her mother didn't have real friends – just a few acquaintances who were probably feeling sorry for her. She determined she was not going to find herself, at nearly fifty, so short of people to love and be loved by. In fact, she felt so strongly about it that she wrote in her journal, "Note to self at fifty – focus on friends and laughter." and then of course, forgot all about it in the repacking to catch a train northwards. She left home on the 30th and changed trains at Preston. From there on the scenery amazed her.

It was a chilly, breezy day, but bright with wintry sun and they crossed a few large rivers and caught glimpses of the Irish Sea away on the horizon. After the pulled out from the shadow of Lancaster Castle the gentle, wooded farmland began to get hilly and these hills were covered in purple heather. The sheep were scattered about, but not so very high and a lady sitting by her, a local, told her they kept them off the tops in winter. She never did discover how they did this. Not long afterwards, they were approaching the grey stone buildings of Penrith where Myra's older brother, Mike, was meeting her.

Chapter 9

She got off the train, with her small case and looked both ways and then walked towards the exit. There were no young men around looking as if they were meeting anybody. But under the archway, where she stood, out of the chill breeze. *What do I do now?* she wondered.

At which point a very elderly and muddy Land Rover careered down the station approach and a raven-haired young man jumped out and hit the ground running.

"Hi," he said holding out his hand. "And you have to be Ella. For God's sake, don't let Myra know I was late. I'll have no peace."

With which he picked up her case and opened to door, swept a few crisp packets from the passenger seat and ushered her in.

"Had a good journey?" he enquired and she told him how great the views were.

"Well, you're in God's country now, Ella." he grinned. He had a really infectious smile and she smiled back. "We're only ten minutes away," he said, "and Cara has given you her room and she's bunking in with Myra. I shall be hag-ridden all weekend." but he grinned again as he said it.

They had no sooner left Penrith and had climbed a little when they were in a small and very attractive village, built around a big green area, which contained a few large trees. As they pulled up at a solid detached house, the red front door opened and Myra ran down the path.

She wore a long rust-coloured corduroy skirt and a cream sweater and looked glowing.

"Ella, how absolutely terrific to see you. Come in, come in." and she ran Ella up the stone path and bundled her inside. Mike followed with her case.

The very first impression was of warmth. There was a fireplace in the actual hallway, a large one which obviously doubled as a dining area. A log fire was crackling away and a door opened and a slightly older version of Myra appeared. The only difference was that this girl had her hair in a loose ponytail.

"This is Cara," as she spoke the girl stepped forward and gave Ella a quick hug.

"I've heard such a lot about you." She stepped back to the door, which seemed to open into a kitchen and shouted in a most unladylike way. "Mum, Ella's arrived." They heard a door slam and then a small, rosy lady came out of the door into the hall.

"OK, I am sorry, I was buried in the freezer. Welcome, Ella. I'm Mum."

"Come on," said Myra. "I'll show you your room. Cara has moved in with me."

"So I've heard, thank you Cara," and Ella took her case and followed Myra up the solid oak staircase."

Her room was a girly delight with a fantastic view out from the rear of the house.

Myra told her that the parents had an en suite and they shared the bathroom next door. Then she sat on the bed and began to gossip. Tomorrow evening the whole family and a few friends had tickets for a hog roast and barn dance to let in the New Year. They had a minibus arranged from their house, where they were meeting up for a drink first. It sounded so different to anything Ella had known and she felt excitement tingling.

"I quite fancy one of the boys, but don't let on to anyone, and, anyway, I'm going to play it cool." Myra told her.

"What is he like then? Tall, dark and handsome?" teased Ella.

"Actually, no, he's quite short and he has red hair and freckles," and they both fell about laughing. Red hair and freckles was supposed to be a big no-no.

A voice floated up to then, "Dinner on the table in about 15 minutes."

"OK, Mum." shouted Myra. "I'll just leave you to freshen up, then," and off she went.

Ella had a quick wash and unpacked. She changed her shirt and brushed her hair and applied a lick of gloss to her lips. She'd never had her ears pierced, but she enjoyed earrings and she popped a pair on before going down. There were sounds of life from the previously used door, so she tapped on it and someone shouted to come in.

The door opened into a really large kitchen, with a great solid pine table running down the middle. It was set for six with a line of pine cones and ivy running down the centre and green glass catching the light.

Standing by the sink was a slim man of medium height with the raven black hair he had passed on to his son.

"John Reid – welcome to our home, Ella."

She guessed he was no more than about fifty and his wife smiled up at him.

"John only works just up the road." she said. "Most days, he walks."

"Do you take a drink, Ella?" someone said in an accent she hadn't heard before.

"Yes, I do. I don't actually drink much." she blushed as she spoke and Myra said, "Well, not often, anyway." and they all laughed.

What a happy group they seemed crowded together between the Aga and the table.

"Here's a nice Fino sherry," John said. "Let me know if you approve."

The drink was cooler and sharper than she had expected, having been raised to drink Bristol Cream. She sipped at it before she decided that yes, she did like it and John watched and nodded his approval.

They all sat to eat and she was between Myra and her father.

Mum's name turned out to be Janice and that was what she was to be called. John, as he told her, was the manager of an animal food mill just out of sight over the hill. He'd been there all his life after doing a course in Accountancy at college. It came a good second best to his family and he acknowledged his luck. Janice worked part time at the village school, doing all the paperwork. If they weren't very careful, they said, they could run most of their lives within a mile of where they now sat. So they made sure they didn't stagnate.

He played golf at Penrith and she was a voluntary fundraiser for Macmillan's nurses. There was quite a lot going on in the area – concerts and such like and they also loved to travel.

"And what about you, Ella?" asked Janice.

"Well, I live in Corby, East Midlands and I'm an only child. My father is in the building trade and Ma works part time in an office. I'm on the same course as Myra."

"Yes, I know that dear, Myra's told me about her flatmates. You all sounded a good bunch and now we've met you I can see you are. It's such a help when you first leave home if you find instant friends. You had a big of a struggle, Cara, didn't you?"

"Didn't I half," re-joined Cara. "I just felt really out of it for ages and missed this lot. I've no idea why." she teased.

But Ella could see why. There was such an easy, teasing but loving atmosphere that anyone in their right mind would miss it.

They had a rich chicken casserole, followed by sticky toffee pudding, apparently a local delicacy. It was all delicious, and a glass of Pinot Grigiot went down a treat.

They all sat happily chatting around the table before Mike said, "I'll fill the dishwasher and then I'm off to Jack's for a quick Young Farmers' meeting," and he went. The rest of them drifted into the big room that ran from front to back of the house. The curtains were drawn and there was a wood-burning stove glowing on a slate hearth. There were two big deep sofas and a few odd comfortable chairs. Ella noticed, because she did take note of such things, that, whilst they were covered they all had the same theme colour, a very deep turquoise. The carpet and the curtains were a sort of cinnamon and there were loads of cushions and footstools about. All in all, a really tasteful family room.

"Television or cards?" asked John.

"Do you play cards?" Janice enquired.

"Nothing too brainy, like bridge, but yes, I play rummy and whist and things."

"And Strip Jack Naked," laughed Cara, and Ella grinned. The evening raced by until Janice went out and came back with a plate of fruit cake, and mugs of hot chocolate.

"Well, I'm off," she said. "It'll be a late one tomorrow, no doubt." John followed here and the girls were not long after. Just as Ella was settling to sleep she heard the sound of the Land Rover returning and smiled to herself. *All in and accounted for*, she thought.

The sounds of door and voices woke Ella at about 8 am. It was a

29

beautiful frosty morning and she could hear a dog barking. As she went down a Golden Retriever came out of the kitchen door, wagged its tail upon seeing her and turned back.

"I didn't know you had a dog." she commented to Mike, who had been lolling on a chair with his feet on the rail of the Aga.

"No, I picked her up last night from Jack's. She's been there for a day or two being introduced to Watkin," he grinned. Ella was now totally bemused.

"Who's Watkin, what do you mean?" she asked.

"Watkin is a fit boy Golden Retriever and we'd all like Goldie to have his babies." At this point he really grinned when he saw she was bemused.

"Oh, you mean you've had her mated."

"Well, she prefers to think she's been on honeymoon," and he laughed at her discomfort.

"Do shut up, Mike," said his mother, flicking him across the head with a tea towel.

"How about eggs and soldiers, Ella, and some Marmite?"

"Wonderful. Can I help?"

"Yes, you can, lass. Will you make the toast fingers for me and put them in that flat basket? Mike, give your sisters a shout. I can hear Dad on the stairs."

Because it was a holiday, everyone was home and they had a carnival breakfast.

"Anyone coming for a walk with Goldie and I?" John enquired.

"Could I?" said Ella.

"Wonderful, anyone else?"

But it seemed not. Myra was giving Mum a hand for tonight's drinks, Cara was having a beauty afternoon following a long soak and Mike was helping prepare for the barn dance.

"Have you got wellies, Ella – no – well, there are all sizes out in the back porch. Are you up to a good old ramble? You look fit enough."

And off they went. He was not an over-talkative man, just making a point of showing her various things along the way and they soon found themselves on the banks of a noisy little river. It was a wonderful walk along what she was told was the River Eden and they went to look at an ancient churchyard on a slight rise above the river.

"They reckon there's been some sort of chapel here since just after the Vikings left." John told her. He laughed. "You look like one of the descendants yourself, with your height and such blond hair. The pigtail emphasises it." and they both smiled.

"Actually, my Da always said we had Viking blood but I always took it with a pinch of salt." Maybe it was true.

"Are you talking of your father in the past tense, Ella? Has he died?"

She took a deep breath. "No," she said, "He just left."

"I'm sorry, that must be rotten," and they carried on in a comfortable silence.

Goldie was off her lead and covered miles more than they did, up and down the banking, sniffing and exploring. She ignored the few sheep they encountered other than a sharp bark.

"Luckily, she isn't a sheep chaser," her master said.

There was homemade soup and warm rolls waiting for them when they got back. In the kitchen were some trays covered in cling film and there were lovely fat candles all over, just waiting to be lit. By 5:30 they were all dressed and buzzing and soon after their guests began to arrive.

Ella had brought her favourite winter coat, a charity shop find, an ankle-length damson velvet, which she paired with an old, soft paisley shirt in cream and damson. Cara had put tiny plaits into the sides of her hair and pulled them together with a piece of gold ribbon and left the rest of her flaxen hair loose. She felt pretty. She never spent much on clothes, or anything really, as she was very wary of building up a huge debt.

The boy Myra liked arrived with his parents. He had a lovely head of coppery curls and looked about 16. Myra more or less ignored him, but he chatted away amiably to everyone else.

The house looked wonderful, with all the candles lit and the big tree ablaze with fairy lights in the hall. The friends all knew each other well and were very welcoming to Ella and there was a happy buzz of conversation amongst the clink of glasses and the sounds of appreciation when the nibbles were brought out.

All too soon, the minibus arrived and they all grabbed coats and, with much hilarity, boarded the bus. Myra and Ella sat together and

Myra gave her a little tour talk. After about 15 minutes they drove through an enormous gateway. It was, of course, in total darkness, but the road lead through some trees and Ella saw a few pairs of eyes glinting in the dark.

"Deer," said Myra. After about half a mile the road ahead went through wrought iron gates with a large 'Private' notice and they saw light in the distance. This, apparently, was where the Lord and his extended family lived. This family had been there for many a hundred years and owned the whole area around, village, forest and land. This was the estate Mike worked on, as it turned out, as an assistant to the Head Gardener.

Within a few more minutes they saw the dim shape of a church tower and then into a slight dip in the line. In front of them was a long low building – a real old coaching pub, The Kestrel. Outside was a Christmas tree covered in tiny white lights and there was a feeling of a haven, which had received many a traveller in its time. They all piled out and into the bar of the pub, already pretty busy. There were shouts of "welcome" and joking familiarity all around. Ella was a little bewildered, until Mike appeared at her side.

"Come and meet some pals," he said to her, and from then on she was fine.

The bar gradually filled up, so that they were all shoulder to shoulder and it began to be great fun. It was New Years' Eve, when people set out to have a good time and it was a real party atmosphere. It seemed that the supper was laid on in about 10, but they began to drift out of the back door and into the huge barn, which had been decorated with strings of hops and holly and mistletoe and ivy. Mike explained it had all been gathered in from the surrounding estate.

"Even the hog only lived down the road," he jested.

In the centre of a long wall was a small stage where the folk band were tuning up and before long they were off. It reminded Ella of some of the music her Da had played on his ukulele and the dances were familiar. Very soon, they were all up and dancing, even the mums and dads, only collapsing when they ran out of breath. *It was so exhilarating and you didn't need a proper partner*, thought Ella. Everyone just joined in.

There was an extremely tantalizing smell drifting in from

somewhere and after a final wild dance the band pleaded a break and somebody shouted, "Food's ready!"

Through a door at the end of he barn they all tramped into a flag-paved yard that was covered along the side. *This was where the smell emanated from and it made you so ravenous,* Ella thought. Myra seemed to be getting on well with her red-head, who turned out to be Andrew, a student at nearby Lancaster Uni. They dragged Ella with them to long trestle tables laid out with barn cakes and pickles, coleslaw and jacket potatoes.

"Fill your boots," said Andrew, so they picked up plates and queued for their sizzling hot slices of meat and crackling.

Then the older folk went back into the warmth while the youngsters huddled on logs and stools around the two big chimneys. Above them, in a black sky, millions of stars were twinkling. Mike came and sat close to Ella.

"I've never seen a sky like this. It is so beautiful, it makes you feel insignificant. Isn't it wonderful?" she enthused to Mike.

"Absolutely." he replied. "It's really great tonight because there is only a sliver of moon and, of course, we are miles away from street lighting. Some folk never get to see a sky like this."

While they sat cricking their necks upward one of the stars seemed to fall from the sky and Ella gasped.

"They're just shooting stars," Mike told her. "Anyway, we'd better eat our meal, or the poor hog will have died in vain." and they set to.

After a couple of minutes of silence, he said, "This is the sort of reason I can't work under a roof. I'm not thick, but I could never work in an office like Cara or sit and study for hour after hour. I need to be out in the open. I think Dad might be a little bit disappointed in my career choice, but he's never gone on about it. I don't earn much, but at the moment, I don't need much. I cough up a bit to Mum and buy petrol and enjoy life. What about you? What do you want out of life?"

Ella thought deeply for a moment, her chin on her hands. "Well, I would hope to find a job where I can be in touch with beautiful objects of all shapes and sizes and then I want to love somebody and marry and have children; but not for ages yet."

"Have you anyone in mind?"

"Good God no, I'm only 19, I'm in no rush," and they both grinned.

"Meanwhile, let's go dance again," and they did.

Then, as midnight approached the whole gathering made a circle and sang "Auld Lang Syne" as the group counted down. They ran out to hear the bells on the old church chime in the New Year and Ella had never been kissed or hugged so much in her whole life.

Janice hugged her. "Happy New Year, Ella. We're so glad Myra has you for a friend."

Ella decided that this was the best night of her whole life one she would never forget.

Mike found her and they kissed each other and wished each other well. "Keep in touch," Mike said. "Give me your mobile number when we sober up in the morning."

"I don't actually have a mobile." she confessed and he thought she was teasing him. When he realised that she meant it, he made her promise to treat herself. "You really need one, you know, if only for your own safety."

"OK, I will, I have been thinking about it," and they stood together enjoying the merriment.

Chapter 10

The next day, everybody was subdued and slumped around watching TV. Ella packed her back and retrieved the good bottle of Chablis she had brought with her. In the evening, she gave it to Myra's parents, as she thanked them for a wonderful couple of days.

"You're welcome any time." they said and she knew they meant it.

Myra confessed that she and Andrew were now an 'item', although they wouldn't see much of each other for a while. Cara was just setting off to her office, as Ella was leaving and told her she hoped to see her again and off she went for the train with Myra and Mike.

Quick hugs followed. "See you in Bristol." said Myra and they all waved as the train pulled away.

Two weeks later, they were back in halls, Ella now the owner of her own phone. She felt she never again wanted to go back to Corby – the time with the Reids had really unsettled her.

Myra was full of Andrew and what he had said and what they had done and Ella said, "Do be careful. You've three years to finish your course yet. Don't throw it all away." She was only trying to talk sense, but she sensed that Myra was a bit offended and they were a bit cool for a while, but it soon blew over.

Jackie went off on her first real 'dig' somewhere in the Black Mountains. She came back saying she would choose a summer dig in future, preferably in Greece, but they could tell she loved it, because she talked so much about it all.

She hadn't mentioned her tutor for a while but now she did. It had burned out was her expression. She had found out he was married and had been given the old story about not being understood anyway she'd met this bloke who was helping on the same dig. They all breathed again.

Myra and Ella were having lectures on textiles and wool and began to learn how to card raw wool. Later, they would learn dyeing techniques and, eventually, spinning.

There were plenty of art shops and small galleries in Bristol and they spent some of their spare hours window shopping and looking at paintings and sculpture and they felt that their tastes were developing.

As the weather warmed, they sometimes took picnics down by the Quay and enjoyed looking at the solid old buildings down there and soaking up the history. They learnt about the Slave Trade that had made Bristol such a rich port along with Liverpool and Lancaster, and then its slow decline. It wasn't long before their first year exams were upon them and the end of their year in halls. They went to the Student Union and collected details of places to rent. They had decided to stick together and try to get something near to the Quays and they found a small terrace house with three bedrooms that they could afford. They decided that they only needed one downstairs room and the small kitchen and drew lots for who wanted a room downstairs. Then they clubbed together to find a deposit and secured a rental for two years. It was furnished with all the necessaries and even had a tiny back yard – their patio it became!

She and Mike spoke every now and then and he declared that he was going to visit their new abode, on his way, with two pals, to Newquay for a lads' holiday.

Meanwhile, Joanne's auntie Wyn had died and her flat was empty, awaiting redecorating and a bit of modernisation before being sold.

Would anyone like to join her there in July? There was no rent and they could self-cater and it was near to the front at Hove. Myra decided to go home. Apart from anything else she missed Andrew, but both Joanne and Ella thought it was a great idea.

But what about Ma, thought Ella, guiltily.

She talked about it with the others and they came up with an idea. When term finished, Myra and Joanne and Jackie were, initially, returning home. "Why didn't Ella invite her mother down to Bristol, for a week or so?" They could have the house to themselves and might suit her mother, whom they all knew was hard work. It took a few calls, but then, suddenly, her mother agreed.

"Yes, Ella, I'd like that."

Ella was quite stunned. She cleaned up and bought some flowers before she met Ma off the coach. She looked different somehow.

She's had her teeth done, thought Ella, and that wasn't all. She wore her pashmina over a cream suit and she actually had a little make up on.

"You look great, Ma," Ella said, genuinely impressed.

Her Ma said, "And so do you," and gave her a brief kiss.

She approved of their little house and she and Ella actually had a good week together. The explored the city and had a cruise on the river, something Ella had never thought of doing. They had a couple of meals out and walked to the Quays one evening to sit outside drinking coffee. It was the best time Ella had ever spent with her mother ever. Her Da was only mentioned once.

On their last evening together, Ma told her she had become 'friendly' with the dentist she worked for and that they sometimes had a meal, or a trip to the cinema. "He's a widower," she confided, "a few years older than me and he has a daughter who's married, living in Norwich."

As Ella tried to digest this information, she added, "There's nothing else to it, Ella, we're just friend, but I mentioned it to your Da when he rang."

"What did he say?"

"It was now none of his business," he had said, "and good luck to you."

He was still on his own.

"Have you still no address for him, Ma?" she asked.

"No, none at all, but I think he's somewhere in the South," and they left it at that.

Chapter 11

Ella was confused, but glad at the improvement in her Ma. She felt more and more that she had a life independent of what her parents did. She had her studies, her little home and a few good friends. That was all she needed.

The girls eventually met up in Hove. The apartment was large, but very outdated although it was comfortable and had obviously once been rather elegant. The aunt had been 94 when she died and a widow for many years. They had a great time there. Mostly the weather was good and a lot of time was spent sunbathing on the pebbly beach and messing about in the sea. On cooler days they explored the 'hoves', a wonderful network of slopes, ranging from the weird to the wonderful and had the occasional pub meal. Once or twice they were invited for a meal at the home of Joanne's parents, who were very hospitable, if a little stuffy. They lived at the posher end of Hove and Joanne had one older brother, much older and long since married and living in Geneva where he worked as a financier. They spoke of him in tones of almost reverence. He had obviously done well for himself.

One night, they went down on the front for the huge annual beach party hosted by Fat Boy Slim and what a rave that was. They had a bit of a laugh with some boys down from London for the weekend and Ella found herself sitting behind one of the groynes with one of them, Charles. They had a bit of a neck and it was quite enjoyable, but when he tried to get a bit too familiar she wriggled away and said, "Whoah, boy, we're not going there."

"Come on, it's all a bit of fun."

"No." she said. "This has been fun, but I don't go further."

"You're on the pill, aren't you?"

"Not that it's any of your business." she laughed, because she knew he was feeling randy and she didn't want to upset him. "But no, I'm not actually."

"My God." he said. "You're a virgin." and he took her by the shoulders.

Her silence spoke for her.

"Well, bloody hell, I must have found the only virgin in Brighton beach tonight." with which he gave her a smacking kiss on the lips and pulled her to her feet. "Let's dance." and they did.

It was the small hours of the morning before they met up again with Joanne and a few others and they made their bleary way back towards the flat, the lads going part way with them. Of Jackie and one of the gang there was no sign. Ella and Joanne sat up with mugs of chocolate, hoping she'd appear soon and she did.

"Quite a night," Joanne said. "I think I'll stay in bed all day tomorrow." and they all agreed.

Sitting quietly watching a DVD the next evening, Jackie confessed she had gone a bit too far with Adam, the boy she'd gone off with.

"It just seemed to happen," she moaned.

The other two girls looked at each other over her head.

"It'll be OK," they said reassuringly and it wasn't mentioned again, when she sent them both text messages.

"All's well, you're not going to be an auntie!"

Ella had always known she wouldn't want that sort of casual sex with anyone. She wanted her first time to be with somebody so special that she would want to be theirs forever. This wasn't a very common ideal amongst the crowd at Uni, but she just stuck to her guns. She had no intent on taking the pill 'in case'. There would be no 'in case'.

By mid-September they were all in their house and together again. Myra was missing Andrew badly and Jackie was seeing someone she'd met at the Union. They began to do more things as individuals, although their friendship was as strong as ever.

Mike rang her a few times. He had decided to go on a course at the local Agricultural College and had got a leave of absence from his gardening job, which was at its quietest in the winter anyway. He'd met a girl and was realising his salary wouldn't go far if he wanted to strike out on his own. She was a second chef in a hotel near Ullswater and lived in, but she hadn't got much cash either. She was called Mary and came from Northern Ireland. Like him she was a volunteer on call for the North Lakes Rescue Team.

Ella was glad to hear he had plans, as she could see he was a bright young man and he talked very fondly and proudly about his girl. Myra said she hoped to meet her when she was home for Christmas and told Ella that her parents had wondered if Ella would like to join them.

There was nothing Ella would like better, but she wanted to give it some thought. She knew there was no spare bedroom and when she stayed Cara and Myra had shared. What if Mike wanted Mary to stay over, or Myra had plans for Andrew? She had such an incredible time with them over New Year and she didn't want anything to spoil that memory. Christmas was different and she might feel in the way, wonderful they all were. Might her presence annoy Mary? There was a lot to consider.

In the end, she thanked Myra with all her heart, and her parents too. She explained why and could see that Myra understood.

"I'll see if Ma wants to come down here for a few days," she told Myra. "I enjoyed her company a lot more during the summer." It was left like that.

Chapter 12

The coursework was more intense and they were all busy with their studies. Sometimes, they would have people in for supper and everyone joined in and brought things to eat and drink. Life rushed by.

Ma hesitated when Ella mentioned Christmas. "I'll call you in a day or two.

And she did. She had plans for Christmas Day, but how would it be if she came to Bristol for a couple of days between then and New Year? Charles would drive her down and they would book a hotel close by. Ella was dumbstruck, Ma had certainly moved on.

"Well, OK Ma, whatever. Let me know just when and where." and she put her phone down on the bed.

Ma must be more than friendly with Charles. Ella didn't want to meet him, but neither did she want to cut the only family bond she had – and what on Earth could she do about Christmas? She was suddenly very, very lonely and sorry for her self. The last thing she wanted was for her pals to be sorry for her and she began to pull herself together. *I need to have something planned,* she thought and suddenly she recalled a poster in the Union appealing for help over the holiday season with soup kitchens for the needy and homeless. Next time she was there, she wrote down the number and once on her own she rang.

"Yes," aid the woman's voice who answered, "They would be very grateful for any help over Christmas. So many students have gone home then that we struggle rather, would you be available actually on the day?"

"Yes, I would," she decided. At least she would be doing some good, even if she would be so alone.

The arrangements were made and she was able to say she had plans and mentioned Ma coming and nobody asked any questions. They were all busy with plans and shopping and then all the and of term parties etc.

She woke one day to an empty house. It was strange, after all the noise and mess. She gave the whole place a good clean and felt quite saintly about that. Then she got changed and went out for a stroll. She located the soup kitchen, which was a fair walk away, and then stopped at a nearby pub for a half of lager. There was a small note on the noticeboard, with a contact number. "Needed – one bright spark to join our Quiz Team." Well at least it would be company - before she could put herself off, she rang and a man answered.

"Oh great - I've only just put that note up in the Ship." he said. "Can you manage Wednesday night? We have pie and chips at 7 and then the Quiz. It's a good laugh, if you like a laugh. Are you good at anything in particular?"

"Well, I'm doing the History of Art at Uni."

"Brilliant, we haven't got anyone arty. How are you fixed for Wednesday next week. My name's Joel, by the way and you must be- ?"

"Ella - Ella Hodson."

"The Ship at 7 o'clock next Wednesday, see you then."

Well, at least she was going to meet some new people in the Christmas break.

She arrived at the pub the next week. It was obviously a popular night, because the place was buzzing. A big bloke stood up as she reviewed the room.

"Are you Ella, by any chance? I'm Joel - Joel Hardacre."

"Nice to meet you," as he guided her back to where he had been sitting. At the table were two people - a slim, dark-skinned man who stood and shook hands and a girl who said, "Hi, I'm Bernie."

The man smiled at her and said, "So you're our new team mate, Ella, and you're arty. Welcome, Ella, we really need you. Joel knows about rugby and the Beatles, and little else." Joel punched his arm. "And Bernie is great on geography, which leaves a yawning gap which I can't fill."

"Some of this lot are hot stuff," Bernie joined in. "Our team is usually near the bottom of the pile. Now listen, boys, tonight we take it seriously. We need to impress Ella. We have a kitty for drinks," she explained, "but none of us drink much. Can't handle it mid-week."

This suited Ella and she happily chipped in some cash. It turned out to be good fun and the time raced by. They had a respectable score and reckoned the new member had earned her place.

"Is it still on next week, with it being between the Bank Holidays?"

"Oh gosh, yes. There's even a special prize. Will you be able to come?" Joel asked.

"Yes, of course. I'll see you then," and with that they began to move.

"Happy Christmas to you all, then," said Joel. "Goodnight."

and Ella walked home in the dark and the drizzle thinking she had made a good move. The other bloke was called Sam and he and Joel were obviously good mates. She knew nothing about them except that Bernie had just been promoted to Staff Nurse at the local hospital and she gathered the boys worked there also.

She treated herself to a little hand made crib set she spotted in a shop window and put up some holly and ivy. With a few lit candles it would look alright, she told herself. Ma and Charles were coming for two nights just before New Year and staying in a small place not far away. She found an old-fashioned watercolour print of the Quays and wrapped it carefully for her Ma. She certainly wasn't buying a present for this dentist man. She dreaded meeting him as it was.

Old habits drew her to Midnight Mass and the carols and the warmth of the church and the old rituals consoled her in a way she wouldn't have imagined. She was early at the soup kitchen and, once started, she never had a minute to even think. There was a huge tree and a warm stove and a constant procession of men and some women. Ella served tea and toast early in the morning, helped to wash up and began to assist half a dozen others with dishing up a good roast turkey meal. Most of their customers wolfed it down, but a few seemed to have little interest in the food. A middle aged man, working alongside said, "They'll be doped up. They've no appetite when they're like that and they're on a downward spiral. We can't do much about it, I'm afraid."

As she began on the clearing up the doors swung open and a large Santa Claus appeared. He strode around with a word for everyone and small identical parcels, that turned out to hold a warm pair of

43

socks.   Some of the men seemed grateful and smiled and thanked him and one little man, who reminded Ella of a mini Santa Claus himself, with his ruddy cheeks and wispy white beard, actually stood up and shouted, "Three cheers for a great meal and a very welcome pair of socks."

Santa departed, taking his bag with him and some short time later, who should walk in but Joel.   "Well, fancy meeting you here.   Did you not recognise me?"

"It was you!   He seemed familiar, but I'd no idea." and she grinned at him.

He bent towards her.   "Merry Christmas, Ella," as his lips brushed hers.

He was on duty now for tea and supper and Ella was free to go, but she didn't rush away.   There was more life here than in an empty house and she liked Joel's company.   He was, she decided that Christmas Day, a gentle bear of a man, someone you could feel safe with and looked forward to getting to know him better.

"Looking forward to the quiz, see you," she called as she left.

It wasn't actually too bad once home.   She lit the candles, put on one of her favourite DVDs of James Stewart in a mushy black and white film about small town USA.   She never tired of it, but never watched it outside of the festive season.   It wouldn't have felt right somehow.   Her mobile rang.

"Merry Christmas, love." It was Da.   "I bet you're having a great time and so you should be, at your age.   Annie told me you were still in Bristol – well, good luck to you."

"OK, Da, happy Christmas and thanks so much for the money. I've spent some of it on a special little crib.   I wish you could see it. I miss you, Da." and she found she had to swallow hard.   "Could you and I meet up sometime – you know – just meet up?"

"Aye, we will one day, meanwhile, take care," and he was gone.

"Damn him," she said out loud, "damn him, damn him, damn him." and she punched her cushion.   How could he just cut himself off from her.   "I will not cry," she poured herself a very large glass of Bailey's and settled down with James Stewart.

The following Wednesday, she learnt a little more.   Joel was from Liverpool, that explained the accent and the quick humour.   Sam's family lived in London.   They were both working as housemen in

Bristol Infirmary. That was how they knew Bernie. Sam and Joel had just qualified and had been together right through Uni, but that might be coming to an end, as Sam was looking for a new job.

Ella was more confident this time and answered a couple of obscure history questions as well as a few in her own subject and they were all pretty pleased with the results.

Over a drink afterwards, Joel asked. "Did you enjoy Christmas Day?"

"Actually, I did, far more than I had expected."

"Good, glad to hear it," but it was discussed no further.

Chapter 13

The next lunchtime Ma duly arrived in a rather nice BMW, with Charles. Ella had dressed up in her best shirt and wore some jewellery. She was going to hold her own with this man.

It didn't turn out like that at all.

"Hello Ella," he spoke in a nice gentle voice and had a pleasant smile. "Your mother has told me how proud she is of you and I'm delighted to meet you."

She showed them in.

"Everywhere looks pretty," her mother said, "and you look very well, Ella. Happy Christmas, dear." and then she inspected the crib approvingly. "Did you have a nice Christmas with all your friends?"

And when Ella said she had it didn't really feel as if she had lied. She ripped open her parcel. It held a really luxurious cashmere sweater, the colour of coral and she loved it.

"Oh, Ma, it's gorgeous. Thank you so much."

Her mother seemed pleased with her watercolour and they sat and chatted with a cup of tea.

"Now then," Charles spoke firmly. "I would be delighted to take two beautiful ladies out for lunch. Any suggestions, Ella, somewhere that would be a treat mind – no student pubs." and she smiled with him.

They ended up a short drive away in a very upmarket bistro, where they had a memorable meal. Ella had never tried scallops before, but did so, on Charles' suggestion and delighted in them. While they ate and drank she studied the man she had been prepared to hate. He was short and stocky, shorter than Annie and his hair was nearly white. He had good square hands, Ella always studied hands, and a kind, ordinary sort of face. Nondescript, she supposed, but she sensed a depth about him.

When her mother went of to 'powder her nose' as she put it, he leaned towards Ella. "This can't be easy for you, but I'm growing fond of your mother and I hope we might, one day, be friends. I'm a widower, my wife died in an accident nearly fifteen years ago. And we had just one daughter. I'll be good to Annie." he told her.

It was easy to believe he would be and her Ma was so changed. *She must have been really unhappy with my Da,* Ella pondered, *and he with her.* It was so sad. They must have loved each other once, though.

Ma came back. "We're in a very comfortable small hotel, Ella. Would you like to join us for afternoon tea tomorrow? It's far too cold and miserable for much sight-seeing."

"We'd both like that very much," Charles spoke and Ella found that she wanted to see them again.

He drove her home and told her he would collect her the next afternoon and he did. While she was sitting beside him she said, "I must say my mother seems a little less critical of me than she used to be. You've made an improvement there."

He gave a short laugh. "Yes, I know she can be a bit outspoken sometimes, but she was unhappy, Ella. I hope she's happier now. She is very, very proud of you even if she doesn't make it obvious." and they pulled up. *I wonder if they share a room,* wondered Ella, but then tried to put it out of her head. After all, they were in their fifties – he was certainly older than Da.

She never before had a proper afternoon tea and they even had a glass of champagne. There was a very large platter of dainty sandwiches and Ella ate her fair share, encouraged by Charles. "You're very young and they all have to be paid for," he said teasingly. There was a fancy cake stand filled with tiny fondant and meringues, fruit tarts and slab cakes. Even the pots of tea were special.

"I can't say how much I've enjoyed myself, thank you so much." and Charles gave her a light peck on the cheek.

"We'll see you soon," they both chorused as they left her at her door.

"I'll probably never eat again," Ella lay on the sofa in front of the fire and read. She had like Charles. But why had Da not been able to make Ma happy? This New Year was a quieter one, but she was fine. She enjoyed her own company, always had, and she wrapped up and walked down to the Quays to let in the New Year. Another year gone and she was almost halfway through her degree course.

Although, Myra had rung her over the hols and she was bursting with news. Andrew had asked her to marry him and Mum and Dad had agreed, but they wanted her to finish her degree. Andrew was in his last year and would be job hunting by summer – and then, next year, they would marry.

"It seems so long off, but I suppose it will be busy, won't it?" asked Myra.

Ella threw her arms around her. "OK, Myra. I'm so really, really happy for you." she said. "I think you have a good 'un there."

"So do I, Ella. I do love him so very much. I'll even be happy to go wherever his job may take him."

"Why?" Ella asked. "Is he planning to go away?"

"Well, his field, or should I say ocean," she laughed, "Of marine biology could take him anywhere. I could be one of those travelling wives." At which they both fell about in a warm embrace.

The quiz nights became a regular date on the calender. One evening, Bernie asked if she knew anyone who would fill in for her while she did six weeks on nights.

Ella asked Myra first, but her head was too full of wedding plans and Andrew to want to be bothered so she asked the other two girls.

As Joanne rightly pointed out, they didn't need another medical person and Jackie said she'd step in. Jackie seemed to get on with absolutely everyone and her Geology was useful too and it became a night the both looked forward to.

Joel, they knew, came from Liverpool and was a "Rugger Bugger". Sam was from a totally different background. His parents lived in Hampstead and had come to England in the 1980s to escape the regime in Uganda. He had a sister and they had been born in London, although in his sister's case it was only just. He worked in the department of Oncology, which Ella didn't know much about. He and Joel, now an houseman on A and E, had been pals now for a few years. They seemed so different to the girls. One was large and extroverted and very funny and the other very much slighter and quieter, although they gradually discovered that he had quite a wicked sense of humour. During the nights together at the Ship Inn, they chatted about their courses and aspirations. Joel wanted to go back North. He liked Bristol and it reminded him of home, being built on sea trade, but it wasn't his Liverpool and it didn't even have a "proper bloody football team" even though his sport was rugby. He explained this that every child born in Liverpool is baptised either a Red or a Blue. His family, apparently, were Blues, except for two renegade brothers.

There were two girls and four boys.

Chapter 14

Jackie didn't want to be stuck in a museum. She wanted to use her degree to find a position that would give her a chance to travel. Outfields, gas fields, that sort of thing.

Sam just said he wanted to learn all he could and try to become the most knowledgeable cancer specialist in his field and Ella dreamt of spending her days in a museum, or a gallery surrounded by beautiful objects and able to arrange and catalogue them. She wouldn't mind working in a good auction house, with lots of art and antiques. There were lots of openings in her line.

Shortly Bernie returned and Jackie retired gracefully, on the understanding that she was number 1 sub. It was all very amiable.

One evening, back at home Jackie said, "You do know Sam fancies you, don't you?"

Ella knew nothing of the sort. "What do you mean, fancies me?" she enquired.

"You've really no idea with men, Ella. It's the way he watches you all the time."

At the next quiz evening she tried to watch him watching her, which was all a bit complicated. He did seem a decent, gentle sort of person and she liked him but she thought Jackie was imagining things.

Very soon after, Sam announced he was going up to Bath for an interview as he was nearing the end of his contract. Suddenly Ella realised how much she had enjoyed these evenings and hated the thought of them coming to an end. Naturally, they all wished him well, but secretly, she thought, *He may not get it.*

But he did. In June he would be taking up a senior post in Bath and he'd be gone.

They all came out of the pub that evening and Sam stayed close to her side.

"Would you mind if I walked with you tonight?" he quietly asked.

"No, not at all, Sam. That would be fine."

They strolled along until some youths pushed past them and he grabbed Ella's arm and he just held it lightly and she found herself enjoying the feel of his arm on hers.

"Would you like a coffee, Sam," she asked when they reached her door, but he declined, probably because of all the lit windows and Joanne's land sheet blaster.

"Perhaps you'd have some supper with me before I go."

"I'd love that. Thank you. How long before you finish?"

"About three weeks. Would Saturday 8 o'clock be alright? I can come here for you, no I know where you are."

"I'll look forward to it. Goodnight, Sam."

"Goodnight, Ella. Saturday, then."

She made a big effort on Saturday, both with her choice of clothes and some light make up. She had to admit to herself that this evening was very important to her.

It turned into a really memorable night, and by the time Sam walked her home she felt herself falling in love, even though she had always laughed at love at first sight. He took her to a really upmarket Italian and he booked a table near the huge window, but in a quiet corner. In between eating and drinking they were able to watch the loud street some and she found they were making up stories for people going past and laughing a lot.

They talked and talked that first evening, until they began to feel they had known each other for years.

Their backgrounds were so dissimilar. Sam's parents were obviously quite well off and still followed their religion, but had adapted very well to living in Great Britain and didn't try to force their beliefs on either of their children. Sam's sister, he said, was half and half, as was her husband, whereas Sam had no belief in any one religion, although he felt there was something superior to us. He lived his life by his own conscience, not being told right and wrong by ministers or anyone, for that matter.

"As long as I never feel I have harmed another being, human or animal, that does me."

Ella told him about her strict Catholic upbringing.

"So how do you feel now?" asked Sam .

"A bit like you, although I still pray to Our Lady."

"Well, I'm sure that does no harm." and the both laughed. As they walked back, on a long summer evening it was the most natural thing in the world to hold hands and, this time, he did come in for a coffee.

The twins and Joanne were out and Jackie made herself scarce. They sat in the kitchen, not wanting the evening to end, and when, reluctantly Sam stood up to go, he said, "A goodnight kiss, Ella?" and he held her face in his brown hands and kissed her long and gently full on the lips.

"Let's make it soon," he said, and they did.

The next couple of weeks flew by and they met up at every opportunity. Sam was going into a B&B in Bath until he found what he wanted. He told Ella his parents had offered to buy an apartment for him, as they had already put a big sum towards his sister's home in Devon. With that in mind he wanted to be sure of choosing the right place.

By the time of the last quiz night, Ella and Sam were an item and being teased about it. Joel was going to miss him too and he promised to take Ella up to Bath the first chance they had, because, of course, both the boys were on a shift system and Joel, in particular, worked very long hours.

Ella and the other girls agreed it was a good job he was such a strong and healthy lad, as A&E wore out a lot of young doctors. Joel seemed to thrive on it – the excitement and variety. He sometimes told them hilarious tales of the mishaps people got into one in particular about the plight of a young chap trying out a sexual manoeuvre had them crying with laughter and then debating for hours whether it was actually possible. You could never tell with Joel he told such a story.

They all got a bit tipsy that last evening and there were promises of reunions etc., but all the time Ella kept thinking – soon he'll be gone.

Once they were on their own again she knew he was thinking the same thing.

"Oh Ella I so wish I wasn't going but I couldn't turn down this opportunity and I didn't know then I was going to be in love."

Her heart leapt into her throat. He had said he loved her she put her arms around his slender shoulders.

"Sam, Sam I love you too. It won't be long before I do my finals and I can find a job in Bath to be near you."

"For always," he said. "Near me for always". And he pushed her gently against the doorframe. His hands slid onto her breasts and he cupped them as they kissed and Ella felt she was melting inside.

"Oh Sam," she groaned. "I want you so much."

She knew he was struggling to control himself and his erection was hard against her thigh.

"But not yet, not here. I want your first time with me to be so special, sweetheart – when we really are 'together'."

And they both slowly pulled back, smiling rather ruefully.

"Soon, then, very soon Sam," Ella sighed.

Once he had gone she threw herself into her last weeks of studying.

Chapter 15

Every day they either spoke or sent texts to each other. He was finding it all very different. He was now a Consultant Oncologist and people actually deferred to him. Joel told her he was one of the youngest cancer consultants in the country. He missed him a lot and he and Ella had the odd supper together.

"Hold on to him Ella, he's a very special man and he'll love you and look after you so well. You two are made for each other. Bagise I'm godfather to the first born."

"Joel, you're rushing the gun a bit," but secretly she was so on fire.

Sam rang one evening. "I've found the perfect place to live. Can you come up to see it before I decide? Ask Joel how he's fixed."

But Joel had no off days due soon so she rang Sam and told him she would catch the bus. Early the next Friday she was on the bus and heading for Bath. It was a lovely ride and she thought to herself how beautiful England was an early summers day. The leaves on the hedges and trees were still a lovely, fresh bright green and the hawthorn was in blossom. They passed apple orchards with all their trees a delight of pink and white and, as the approached the city she noticed how hilly it had become.

Sam was waiting as the bus stopped and held his arms out when he saw her, totally unfazed by the smiling passers-by. She ran to him and into his embrace and the world just stood still. After a minute or two he picked up her bag and said.

"Wait 'till you see what I've got," leading her with his free hand.

They rounded the corner, into a small, short term car park and he stopped. "Well, what do you think, Ella?"

Right in front of them was a low open-topped car in a brilliant fire-engine red. She hadn't known he owned a car and said so.

"No, you're right, I didn't. I've just treated myself. It's a '75 Triumph Spitfire and it does have a top. Jump in." and he threw her bag in behind the seats.

She folded her long legs in and the leather seat held her very comfortably.

Sam revved the engine and laughed. "She really goes if you get some open road. I'll show you later, but first a look at the flat." and they took off fairly sedately, soon running into traffic anyway.

"I still use my bike around town, it's usually pretty bad for traffic. Amazingly, this flat has a designated space for one car, which would be a hell of a bonus."

The city was very attractive in the sunshine, all golden stone and Georgian buildings and Ella was charmed by it. They drove past the famous Royal Crescent, sweeping past a huge grassy area with trees all around.

"Sam, this is terrific. It's so elegant. I bet these houses cost a mint."

"A mint and a half," was the reply as he slid left and began to climb a slope.

Ella was so busy looking all around her that it took her by surprise. They stopped in another crescent, a smaller one than they had just left, but with grass and shrubs and trees between the terrace and the road.

"No 6," Sam said. "Top floor, which means a few stairs, but hey! We're young and fit, and he held his hand out to her as she climbed out of the car.

"The agent should be here soon," and they approached an iron gate, which opened onto a narrow, bricked pathway. Either side of them were formal borders, covered in red geraniums and lots of white flowers. It was all pristine. Sam stopped at a smaller gate set into the wall beside the steps.

"That's a semi-basement and I'm allowed to keep my bike there, if I buy the flat," and they peered down some wide impressive steps and a large solid-looking door, painted a glossy black.

Sam saw her looking and told her that the ground floor was the offices of a company of architects and one of the partners lived on the first floor. As the top floor was underused they had done some work on it and was for sale on a 99-year lease. When he told her how much they were asking, she took a step back.

"Sam, that's a small fortune."

"Yes, I know, it is pricey, but just look where it is. It's just around the corner from one of the most expensive pieces of real estate in the country. I can cycle to work and the parents want me to have somewhere good to live. They're thrilled about my Consultancy and this is their way of showing it. Anyway, wait until you see it before passing judgement – here's the agent now."

After a quick handshake, he drew out some keys and opened the door. They stepped straight into a long, narrow hall floored in large black and white tiles and on the plain white walls were lots of framed, large, black and white prints. The agent set off up the flight of stairs and they followed. There was a dark grey carpet on the treads and along the next area, looking just like downstairs. At the top of the next flight was a square landing area, with a very large mirror on one wall and another black glossy door.

The middle-aged man smiled at Sam. "Perhaps you would like to open up and show your young lady," and he stood to one side.

The first stunning impression was of light and space. The room they stepped into was floored in wood, wide golden planks of polished wood. One entire wall was glass and as she stepped towards it, Ella saw there was a wide metal balcony outside this huge glass wall. She stood absolutely mesmerized by the view before her. It was as if the whole city was spread out.

She turned. "OK, Sam, how breathtaking it is. No wonder you fell for it."

He put his arm round her shoulder. "I just knew you'd be blown away." He looked so happy she wanted to kiss him there and then, but felt too silly in front of the estate agent. He chuckled. "Well, perhaps you'd better have a look at the actual rooms." They both turned from the view and took in the lounge area. At one side was a view of a galley-type kitchen, semi-separated by a serving bar with glass shelving above it. There was just one other door, which lay opened into a wide hallway. From there they went into the kitchen, fitted out in plain white glossy cupboards, with black granite tops and there seemed to be everything you would need in a kitchen, although Ella was so excited she scarcely checked. It was Sam who said, "All you'd need is behind the cupboard doors – including a washer/dryer and a fridge/freezer," he added. "OK, well, that settles it," grinned Sam.

There were three other doors. The first she tried was a large cupboard with hanging hooks, and some shoe racks. Then the bedroom, again a large room fitted with white glossy furniture. There was another door hidden in the row of wardrobes and this was a large and very modern bathroom with access again though to the hall.

"I can't imagine anywhere more perfect, and it's all so new and glossy, Sam, you must have it, if you can afford it. I just love it."

And off she went to have another look at the kitchen and then back to the view. When she returned, Sam was in conversation with the man by the door. She saw them shake hands and Sam turned. "Well, it's done and dusted, Ella. I don't need a mortgage, I've nothing to sell and the owners have provided a full survey. I can be in it a couple off weeks," and they hugged each other tight.

"If you would like I can leave you to let yourselves out. You probably need time to think. I hope you'll both be very happy here," and the agent went.

Ella laughed. "He thinks we're moving in together."

"Well, what a wonderful idea."

"But Sam..."

"Yes, is that a problem?"

"Not a problem at all, but it's so sudden. We don't really know each other very well and I haven't done my Finals."

"No, I realize that, but you will be footloose very soon. As to knowing each other, I know all I need to know and we have the rest of our lives to discover the rest. We love each other, Ella, why waste any time? There's only one life ahead of us, no matter how long. Carpe Diem, Ella, Carpe Diem," and they fell into each others' embrace.

"Well, all that kissing has made me hungry," Sam declared after a few delicious moments, "lunch beckons." and after one more long look around, they left.

"I just can't believe we could be living in such an incredibly wonderful place," Ella went on, "but what will I tell Ma and will I be able to find a job here?"

"Tell your mother the truth, that you are in love and I'll tell my parents exactly the same." He was so certain and so light-hearted about it that her tiny misgivings were soon just a memory.

Over lunch at a pub Sam had discovered, called The Raven, famous for its pies, they talked and talked and talked. How would they furnish the place? When could Ella come again? Questions, questions, questions. The pies were to die for, with wonderful names such as Chicken of Aragon and they went down well with a glass of cider.

Sam told her about his new job and that he just revelled in being in this city. "I know where the furniture stores are, shall we have a look after lunch?"

They didn't need the car, everything was fairly close to hand, although the streets were very hilly, but it was such fun to be exploring it together that they wouldn't have noticed Mount Everest. They had already decided that they must emphasise the space and light of the flat and fell in love with a huge, white leather sofa. It curved sinuously and one end dropped down and they could just see it on the golden floor. That quickly had a 'Sold' sign on it. Sam fancied a glass-topped square coffee table with red shiny legs, but Ella said red would be too obvious, they needed to have a think about colour. "Okay, sweetie, you're the expert," he said and they carried on browsing.

There were a lot of small art shops and galleries, which encouraged Ella to think she would be able to find a position. The afternoon just flew by.

"I forgot to tell you, my landlady can let you have a nice room for tonight. Will that be alright with you? I'm back at the hospital at 2 o'clock tomorrow, so I can put you on the bus before then."

Ella would have slept in a cardboard box just to be near Sam, so the arrangement delighted her, as did the small room back at his B&B. After a quick freshen up they went out for the evening, drifting around and finding the delights of Bath.

I believe there's a rooftop spa pool somewhere around here." Sam said at one point. "Maybe next time." and Ella hugged herself that there would be a next time – lots of them.

With her head buzzing with all the thought it wasn't as bad leaving Sam the next lunchtime. They had a good breakfast and spent a couple of hours looking at ideas. Curtains or blinds? Did they need a table or chairs and then the big one, what about the bed?

Ella found herself a bit embarrassed about the subject of a bed.

After all, they had never gone that far, but it was going to happen, wasn't it? Sam picked up on her unease and teased her gently.

"We love each other, Ella. I've behaved myself up to now, but I'm not going to sleep on the floor, am I?" and they ended up laughing.

Chapter 16

On the bus back to Bristol she made a big decision, and that night, late on, after Sam had finished at the hospital, she rang him. "Sam, I'm going on the Pill," she said, "by next time I see you I'll be safe."

Her pals were amazed. Ella, the quiet one, was throwing caution to the wind. Who would have guessed?

But she sensed they were glad for her. Question followed question. Were they going to move in right away? Had she told her mother? Had they actually 'done it' yet?

"Yes, no and no."

"Well, it's time you did," was the general consensus and she had made the first step.

She wrote to Ma. She couldn't face trying to tell her by phone. A week went by before her mother rang. There were a lot of questions. Who was he, what was his background and what, exactly did he do?

Ella managed to convey all the answers without actually saying that Sam was Asian. Ma was obviously delighted that he was a Consultant and Ella was too happy to want a row. She would leave that for now. She knew how biased her mother could be.

"Is he a Catholic, Ella?"

"No, Ma, but I don't go to church very often myself."

A deep sigh followed on the other end.

"It's all so different now, but you make sure you find a job to go with your degree and keep your independence."

"I will, Ma, perhaps we could all meet when I'm settled in Bath. It's a totally beautiful city. You must come to it," and there it was left.

Soon after, Myra had a call. Mike was actually coming South this year – only a year late – and was calling with his girl.

They went to a pub together and it was good to see him, although Ella wasn't too struck by Mary. She seemed a bit childish and clingy, she thought. He told them about the course he had just finished at Newton Rigg. He was now a qualified green keeper and felt that there were more lucrative openings in golf than in gardens. "People are cutting back on spending on large gardens, they are having to, but golf has really taken off and there are new courses all over the show, as well as all over the globe." His enthusiasm was infectious.

He and Mary were off to have their first holiday together, in a friend's bungalow at Padstow. "Actually, it belongs to his granny, but she lets it out to friends really cheaply," Mike told them.

He wanted to know about her plans, and, obviously, about Sam.

"How do your parents feel about him being Asian?" he asked.

"They don't know yet!" and everyone roared with laughter, all except Mary, who looked disapproving. She reminded Ella, in that few seconds, of her Ma. *Oh Mike,* she thought, *don't make a mistake,* but then the feeling passed.

Very suddenly, their lives in Bristol were coming to an end. Jackie and the present boyfriend were headed for a holiday in Ibiza and Myra thought she had a job in a small art shop in Penrith. By next summer she would be married to Andrew and it filled her waking moments. Joanne had a job lined up as the 'lowest of the low' as she called it, in a hospital at Eastbourne and then would be back for another two years' study.

As for Ella, in a state of bubbling excitement she began to pack her belongings and prepare to move to Bath. Joel had offered to take her there. For one thing, he was curious about the place, having heard so much from her and Sam, and he wanted to see Sam's flat. Also, Sam's car was too small for Ella's worldly goods, even though they were not many.

There was one last tearful and sentimental night in 'their' little house and they all flitted off in different directions, with promises of lifelong calls and friendship. It was all so sad. These years had been the best of Ella's life, although she had joyful anticipation of a lot of happiness ahead of her.

And she wasn't wrong. Joel was gobsmacked at his first sight of the apartment and fell in love with the whole place. The leather suite had been delivered and he accompanied them to look for what he called 'the Marital Bed' with capital letters in his voice. They had such laughs in the process, especially as Joel had a way of intimating that the bed was for all three.   In one shop, Ella thought she would wet herself at his antics.

In the end, the decision was made – a 5ft wide modern black iron bed, with a simple headboard.   It would be delivered in a few days. As there were fitted wardrobes and drawers in the bedroom, they felt they could move in once that was installed.

"What about bedding?" Ella suddenly thought and they all rushed off to find sheets and duvets.   That evening they all collapsed in what was now Sam's second home, his B&B, over fish and chips and pints of local cider.

"If you'd like I could keep an ear open for any jobs coming up here," Sam told Joel and they both agreed that would be great, as did Ella, who thought of Joel as she felt an older brother might be, as he and Sam were both five years older than she was.

He stayed over the next day and Sam hired bikes for Joel and Ella and took them on a wonderful ride along the old Bristol and Bath railway.   Ella had never been so far on a bike, but it was mostly flat and there were lots of sculptures to be inspected en route.   Sam took pity on her and they put their bikes on the train to return.   It was a really exhilarating day and they all had such fun and Ella felt her life opening before her, just like a blossoming flower.

They all ate at The Raven and then, early the next day, Joel had to get back and Sam was due at the clinics he was involved in.   They had breakfast together and decided Sam's next full free day was Apartment Day – they day they would move in together.   It was four days off.

When Sam had got his landlady got quite sentimental about losing him.   She told Ella he had been the loveliest lodger she had ever had and she would miss him so much.

"I believe they love him at the hospital, too," she confided.   "I've a cousin who has recently been diagnosed with breast cancer and she raves over this gentle, kind young Mr Patel."

Ella could have burst with pride and emotion.   She wasn't alone in thinking her Sam was special.   In a rush of emotion she said, "When we're settled, you must come and see us."

Mrs Grey coloured.   "Oh, how I would just love to do that." she said.   "Thank you so much, Ella." and they both went about their business.

Ella decided to try to find if there were any jobs to be had and began to tour the streets, while Sam was at the hospital. She steeled herself to call on every single arty-looking place she passed, and on her first day met with many polite refusals. Towards the end of the second day, a man in a small gallery asked if she had thought of approaching any of the museums.

"Because they are larger, there are always more chances there than in the smaller places," he kindly explained. "Are you newly qualified?"

When she confessed she was, he said, "Here, take my card. I've written the name and mobile number of a pal at the Museum of Costume. He may be able to help." and he told her where to find it.

Bright and early the next day, she was off to the Assembly Rooms. She hadn't mentioned any of this to Sam, and he thought she spent her day window-shopping. She reached her destination, in Bennett Street, and took a few deep, calming breaths. At Reception, she asked to see Mr Steven Asquith and was asked her business. She replied that she had been given his name by the gentleman at the Polluse Gallery and was asked to wait.

It was a long wait and she tried to keep calm and relaxed. Just as she was despairing, the girl called across to her.

"Mr Asquith can see you now – Room 4 on the Ground floor, near the stairs."

Ella knocked lightly. "Come," said a deep voice and she went in.

Her very first thought was, *He looks just right for a museum*, because the man who rose from a leather chair behind a large desk hand long grey hair and a grey Van Dyke beard. He also wore a dark blue corduroy jacket and a bow tie.

"Miss Hodson," he intoned, in that rich voice, "do come in. Sit down, my dear, and tell me what you want of me. I understand my friend has sent you."

She took a deep breath and kept her hands folded, so that they wouldn't shake.

"Well, Mr Asquith, I have just completed my degree in the History of Art at Bristol. I don't have my results yet, but should have done well. My particular interest is in fabrics and textiles and tapestries and I am looking for a position in that sort of field. I have moved to Bath to be near a young man who works at the local hospital and intend to stay here."

Mr Asquith regarded her. "Are you any good with a needle?" he asked.

"Oh yes, sir, I can card and dye and spin," she answered eagerly.

"Do you mind getting your hands dirty?" which was a strange question.

"I just want to work with fabrics with a history and to explore that history and learn and I'll do anything I am asked to do," she replied, quite firmly.

He smiled. "I like what I see and I like what I hear, and, by a wild coincidence there is an opening. It would not be a well-paid job, but there would be a lot of space to learn and progress. Basically, we need somebody within the next few weeks who could clean and repair items given to use before they are ready to display."

He told her the hours and the salary.

"Could you begin in three weeks' time?" he asked. "Our present lady is leaving to have her first child and is going to be a full-time mother – and quite rightly so. Would you care to consider the proposition?"

"Oh, no, thank you?" Ella said. "I would love to say yes now, if that's alright. It sounds ideal." and she smiled at him.

"Well, wonderful – absolute serendipity," and he stood to lean over the desk and shake her hand. He rang an old-fashioned bell and a middle-aged lady appeared.

"Miss Hodson, my dear, our new girl, and I would enjoy a cup of tea." he twinkled. "Miss Hodson, meet Mrs Asquith, my prop and mainstay in both life and work."

Mrs Asquith beamed at her.

"How nice to see a new young face." and she smiled as she closed the door.

Leaving the museum later, after a conducted tour, Ella could scarcely contain herself. She had a job, and not just a job. It was in the very field she had been intrigued by all her adult life and the Asquiths seemed a total delight. She could barely wait until Sam got in. she waited at Mrs Grey's front gate to see him turning in on his trusty bike.

Chapter 17

"Sam, Sam," she gabbled. "I've got a job."

He stood holding his bike. "You've got a job? How? Where?" and he balanced his bike on the fence. "Oh, Ella, my wonderful Ella. What did I do before you? Come in and let's hear all about it." - and he did.

"Right," he said. "A celebration is called for. Tonight, we shall go to The Circus."

He laughed at her expression. "No, not that sort of circus. It's a great restaurant, for treats only, so wear your glad rags," and they tore off to their separate rooms to prepare.

It certainly was a treat and he listened as she told him about what she would be doing. They were both on a high and there was only one day and two nights to go before they moved in together. They talked about the practicalities, but both avoided the thing first and foremost on their minds.

Saturday, or A-for-Apartment Day, was so huge. They arrived at the apartment at 8:30 and the bed was delivered, along with an impulse buy black bookcase. The men had quite a struggle getting it safely up the stairs, but then it was all assembled in a few minutes. They left and Sam and Ella were suddenly alone, in their new apartment, with just a few bits of furniture and Ella became practical.

"Let's make up the bed and see how it looks," and this they both did.

Everything was white and she had bought white luxurious towels as well. Her idea was to live with the black and white until a colour evolved that they would use in all the space. Sam had said she was the arty one and he would leave it to her choice.

The bed looked extremely luxurious, but rather too virginal, when it was done, and Ella felt herself turning pink. Sam saved the day. He had carried in a couple of M&S bags, which he took into the kitchen, and after a bit of rooting about he produced a bottle of rose champagne and a dish of nibbly things. He had also hidden two flutes, wrapped well in tissue paper.

"Let's drink to us, Ella," and he filled their glasses as they stood by the window. "To all our future years together." and they giggled at the idea and drank their toast.

"We haven't any dishes or pans or anything," Ella suddenly said. "We must be mad."

"Yes, we are, and isn't it just wonderful?" and Sam took her empty glass and put it on the wooden floor. "Come here, Ella, while I ravish you."

Amongst a lot of laughter and kissing they both fell back on the huge sofa.

Ella was giddy with excitement and champagne and some other, almost primeval, urge. She pulled open Sam's suit and shrugged it off his brown shoulders and began to kiss him, moving her mouth slowly downwards onto his taut chest. Her instincts took over and she knew what she was doing. Sam, meanwhile, had managed to drag her shirt over her head and was beginning to moan softly.

"Ella, oh, Ella," and then an even deeper moan, as she unzipped his jeans, and dragged them off. She had never before seen a man naked, certainly not in the state she now saw Sam. All her unease had flown out the window and she could only see how beautiful his body was. As she gently took him in her mouth, he groaned again and wrapped his fingers in her hair.

"Oh dear God, Ella – that's so good – come here," and he gently pulled her head up to his. As he kissed her long and deeply on her lips he pulled her onto the white leather and slid her skirt and briefs away. He spread her legs and she pulled her hand onto her flesh and moved it to where she need it it - "There, oh, just there."

His fingers teased her for a moment and then he was kneeling above her and all she wanted was to feel him inside her. She wantonly tilted herself toward him and there was a fleeting sharp pain and then a long slow thrust and he stilled inside her and held her very tightly.

"Are you okay, sweetheart?" he asked her. "Am I hurting you?"

"No, Sam, it's so lovely – I want it, I really want it." and Ella gave her whole love to this very special man.

It was short and fierce and left them both shell-shocked and silent, holding each other so closely. They just lay there, quite peacefully, until Sam spoke.

"Well, I can barely speak." he patted her lightly on her cheek. "What will you be like when you've practised a few times?" and they laughed together so happily. After they'd gathered their thoughts, they decided to finish the champagne and get dressed (in that order) and go off to buy pans etc.

But first they made love again, to make sure the bed worked. This time it was a little slower and very, very sensual and Ella found she was rather rapidly turning from a rather shy virgin into a young woman who was really eager to explore whatever came along. How glad she was that she had waited for Sam. If this was sex it had been well worth the wait.

The shower was large enough for them both, but that lead to another vigorous romp, under the warm water and they were both weak-kneed when they eventually were clothed again.

It was, by now, late afternoon.

"To Hell with shopping," Sam said. "We can eat a takeaway on our knees and have a bottle of wine. Tomorrow we'll do the shops."

So their first evening was spent eating Chinese with plastic forks, watching the sun going down over Bath, drinking wine and planning their futures.

Chapter 18

By 9:15, Gaynor and Ella were back at the cottage. The old house twinkled this morning in the early sun coming over a distant head cloud and, when they got in, they found the kitchen was full of its golden glow. This time, Ella was more practical and had a really good look at everything. The kitchen and bathroom would have to be gutted and actual heating installed. Much as she would love to have fires lit, she didn't want to be reliant on them. Apart from that it all seemed sound. Even the stone outhouse was dry and solid and all sorts of dreams began to pop up in her head. It seemed such a very long time since she had had any dreams. Perhaps it was a good sign.

"Could you arrange a full survey for me?" she enquired. "And what about people to do the plumbing etc. Are there any locally?"

Gaynor smiled patiently at her. "We have all the local tradesmen you need, plus terrific craftsmen too, if you're looking for upmarket. The farthest you need to go for anything is Caernarvon, but it's only half an hour away. We have most things you might need down here on the peninsula."

Ella was getting more and more involved and tried to ask all the right questions.

"Is it freehold?"

"Yes, all of our land is."

"What about doctors and hospitals, dentists and such like?"

"Doctors around the corner, major hospital in Bangor and a dentist in Pwllheli. Did you mention a dog? The vet's hospital is just the far side of Pwllheli." Gaynor laughed. "We even have the RAF helicopter just 10 minutes away, at Valley, for real emergencies. As for a social life, well, it's mostly home made, but all the better for that. There is a cinema in Pwllheli and we often have visiting theatres. There's a huge jazz festival right here in June and, of course, Wakestock, in July. A real madness that is, I can tell you. Look, why don't we have a coffee in the village and talk it over. It's a huge decision, on your own."

So that was where she planned her new life, over a little antique come teashop on the main street. She popped in briefly, to tell Tudor the news and then followed Gaynor to the office. They put her in touch with a local solicitor. It was decided that, all being well with the survey, to see to her side of the transaction, she would take possession early in January.

The small town of Pwllheli was buzzing, in the run up to Christmas and she was greatly surprised at hearing so many people chatting in Welsh. She bought a pasty at a bakery and the ladies switched to speak to her in English, but heavily accented with their native tongue. She hadn't realized before that the people spoke Welsh by choice. She must ask about that, it seemed so strange. She would have more chance of understanding French or Spanish speakers. It was a foreign land alright.

She turned her car South again for her long trip and the night was falling as she left the mountains behind. She ate her pasty on the way and approached Bath by late evening.

Instead of heading home, she drove closer to the hospital, to a block of flats, used to house some of the medical staff. She rang Joel's bell and swept open the door. After a big bear hug, he said, "You've made it, well done. I'm on at midnight. He's all fed and watered and walked."

Then he suddenly remembered. "How about you – how has it gone, Ella?" as he spoke he was ascending the flight of stairs behind her.

She stopped on the landing and, as he unlocked his door, she said, "I liked it, in fact I've bought it subject to survey."

"Wow." he said. "An instant decision. When will you go?"

"In January. There's some work to be done, but I'd like to be there to watch over it, so yes, early January I reckon."

By now they were in Joel's bedsit, a typical pad with TV and DVD and speakers hogging a lot of space. Lying on the brown sofa was a brindle-coloured dog with a sad expression. He slid off the cushions and came to meet Ella. "My, Bones, been a good dog?" He slithered away again and Joel said.

"A nice mug of hot chocolate?"

"OK, have you got time? I'd love one." and she sat next to the dog, who was back on the sofa.

"So, tell all," Joel demanded and she went through her forty-eight hours away. It seemed longer.

"I feel I'm making the right choices, Joel."

"I'll miss you so, Ella, but it seems right for you. Anyway, I shall head North sooner or later. I'm not really cut out for life below Manchester." and they both laughed.

Chapter 19

Back at No. 6, with Bones, she looked around the empty flat. It was so lonely, but it felt so empty. Apart from her treasured tapestry it all seemed perhaps too minimalist – maybe more Sam's taste than hers. She'd given the tapestry pride of place and she loved it. They had started slowly and with great thought begun to buy bits and pieces from their home and she had spotted the piece of art in a local show window and taken Sam to see it.

"Isn't that truly glorious?" she had asked and he nodded slowly.

"I shall buy it for you," he said.

She said, "But I've no idea what it will cost."

"Well, we'll never know if we don't ask," and in they went. Some ten minutes later they came out together carrying a large parcel. It had not been cheap, but Sam said it would prove to be an investment, also they had plenty of cash between them and anyway he wanted her to have it. They carried it home and up the stairs and carefully removed the packaging. It was a 1930s piece of work, all dark greens, lime greens, gold and duck egg blue. It was whatever you wanted it to be – a sky or the sea, or a dream – whatever, Ella just loved it. The frame was simple, narrow and gold. Sam held it against their longest wall.

"Oh yes, just off-centre and I'll find cushions and glass and things to pick up the colours," and, in time, she did.

Sam said she was like a magpie and only arrived home with things to treasure. She found silk and velvet in a stall, which she transformed into covers for big fat cushions for the sofa and the bed. She bought odd pieces of glassware that gave light to the kitchen, all in the colours of her tapestry and she bought a kit and began on a small, abstract work of her own, which she sat with at night. Their happiness was like a huge soft blanket that wrapped them in a glow of love. Sam paid bills and eating out and she bought food and extras. They had a big disposable income, but they worked hard and frequently just stayed in and watched TV or listened to music. Her tastes were a bit more high-brow than his, but they lived a life of give and take. Whoever was home first, or least tired, cooked. Some nights nobody cooked and they had one of the local takeaways. They still went to the pub and had the odd meal out, but they spent a lot of their time making love. They were never too tired for that. They just couldn't get enough of each other and they were on a constant high. Even when they were tired and had decided on a sensible early night, Ella would awake to feel Sam hard against her and she would wriggle her bottom towards him and his hands would slide around her and they would already be hungry.

Mr Asquith commented on her full-time smile and she thought, *If only he knew*.

Some days she still throbbed from the excesses of the night and she loved feeling like that, as if Sam was never too far away.

She was so lucky. Mr and Mrs Asquith were very parental and she felt they cared about her well-being. They asked tentative questions about her boyfriend and she told them things she knew would keep them content. She told nobody about their love life – not even her closest friend, Joel.

Her days were fascinating. She worked in a semi-basement room, with large windows and big worktables, a washing machine, a sewing machine and a young assistant called Sacha. Sheer department, as Mr Asquith called it, received all the clothes donated to the museum and these had to be inspected and washed and ironed, perhaps starched and small tears darned etc. Sometimes things had been purchased, but mostly they were donations after the demise of parents or family. Some of the clothes she worked with were not all that old, but were gems of their era, such as a Mary Quant mini or a Chanel suit. It gave Ella a real kick to see some of her work out on display and, gradually, she was allowed, more and more often, to actually assist in setting up these displays. Her salary increased and she felt very fulfilled.

Sam, of course, had a very different work environment, and his job could be very harrowing. She knew, as soon as she looked at him, if his day had been particularly bad. On these evenings, they just sat quietly together until she sensed the tension leaving him and then they would make a quick meal. He was a stir-fry expert and she was good at pastas, so cooking was quick and enjoyable.

Sometimes, not often, he would lie in her arms and tell her some sad story, but mostly it was just left and their loving in the evenings and nights seemed to give him huge solace.

Joel popped up sometimes. They had a black leather recliner that just about held his big bulk and he would kip for a night or two. She spoke often to Myra. The wedding was June and she told Ella to book the date. Andrew had a possibility of a job on the west coast of Ireland, off the coast of The Dingle. She didn't think Mike was happy with Mary, but didn't want to hurt her. They both heard from Jackie – excited calls. She was off to Thailand with an oil company – a three year contract – cheerio and good luck.

Mrs Grey was asked for lunch one day and was most impressed. "No more than you both deserve." ash she picked her way through a salad mixture strange to her tastes, but delicious.

Joel dropped his bombshell on his third visit. He had tried very hard to be otherwise, but he was gay and he had to tell them first. Sam had thought as much but Ella was devastated. Brilliant Joel, who would make such a great husband and father. She threw her arms around him.

"We love you so much, Joel, and always will. Have you told your family?"

"Well, one of the boys guessed and asked me last time I was home, but no, I haven't, but I will now. Next time I'm back in the Pool I'll pluck up the courage."

After he'd gone back to Bristol, Ella said, "I never would have guessed, Sam."

And he replied. "They don't go all over the top, you know. It makes no different. He's the same old Joel." and on that they were agreed.

Some weeks later, Sam rang Joel to tell him of a post that was in the pipeline, and, to their real joy, Joel walked into it. He moved into a hospital flat and was welcomed at Bath Rugby Club and his cup runneth over.

He'd managed to tell his family, who had turned out to be very supportive, except from one brother and Joel said he could live without his approval anyway.

As their first Christmas appeared on the shy line they debated how to celebrate and they decided to join the carol singing around the wards on Christmas Eve and then Sam would go with Ella to Mass at midnight, a shade reluctantly, but he loved her so he would. As it turned out, he quite enjoyed it all and they walked home, alone, on a bitterly cold night. They had a small tree and Ella's crib and candles lit and a few wrapped gifts under the tree. They were having a late dinner on the day itself, as they were including Joel, who only came off shift at 8pm. They decided to open one gift each before they went to bed.

Ella handed Sam a parcel. Inside was a beautiful caramel shade cashmere sweater, which he held up against him. It was perfect and he said so, as he kissed her. When Ella pulled the wrapping from hers she found an exquisite tapestry bed pull – very obviously many years old. It contained all the colours of the big one on the wall. There was a small label tied to it with cotton. "The Abbey of St Ethelred, c. 1590" she read. It was so lovely and so unexpected she found herself crying. Then, of course, Sam had to make her happy again – and so they saw in the Christmas morning.

A fairly quiet New Year, with Sam on duty a lot of the time, and soon after he had a letter from his parents. They would like to meet Ella and see where he lived and thought they might come to Bath the second week in January. Would that suit him? They jiggled their time off and went to The Royal Crescent Hotel at lunchtime to meet Mr and Mrs Patel. He was obviously Sam's father, just smaller and slighter and a very elegantly dressed man of great charm. She was in a sari with a European twist to it and a very pretty woman. Sam had told her they were in their 60s and they were a handsome pair. They held their hands out to her – both hands and told her how pleased they were to meet her. Then they went in for lunch. Gradually, over a sumptuous meal, they all loosened up and they began to tell her snippets about Sam's childhood and about his sister and Ella talked a little about Corby and her pals in Bristol.

"You seem to have lots of shared interests," Sam's mother spoke, "but you have your own very interesting career. Do tell us more about it." and as she and Ella chatted happily, so did Sam and his father. After a long lunch they arranged to meet up the next morning at the flat and Sam and Ella strolled home.

Chapter 20

"I do hope they like it."

"What's not to like?"

"What's their home like, Sam?"

"Full of nick nacks and ornaments and frills."

"Oh God, they won't like it, will they?"

However, once they had caught their breath, they really did approve. The view, of course, caught their attention, but so did the minimalism and the sharp contrasts of bright colour.

"So easy to keep clean, I imagine," murmured Mrs Patel, "and with you both working hard."

The visit was a success and they showed them a few of the sights of Bath before they left.

"They liked you," said Sam as they lay entwined on the sofa. "But I love you," and he picked her up and carried her into the bedroom and threw her on the bed, That was an evening when they did a lot of laughing and fooling about, but it ended, as it always did, with sex that almost blew their minds.

They decided to arrange a short holiday and they both fancied St Ives. He loved the sea and she wanted to see the Hepworth Gardens and the Tate.

"How about calling on sis on the way there?" he asked one morning, over a quick coffee.

"Fine by me, where are they exactly?"

"In Totnes, isn't to far off our route."

It was sorted. Netta would be delighted to see them. Could they only stay the one night?

They drove down to Devon in the Triumph, with the hood up and the heat on. It was, after all, only March. To their delight, the daffodils were in full flower as they went South and Totnes was a delightful place of medieval buildings on the River Dart.

Netta and Rav's house was a white painted cottage in the middle of a row of five and about 100 yards from a bridge over the river.

Sam blew his horn and his sister flew out to meet him, just like his mother but in jeans and a warm sweater. She waited as Ella clambered out and then she kissed her on both cheeks and said, "So you are the famous Ella who bas made my kid brother such a happy man." and she stood back to usher them in.

The cottage was like the TARDIS, with one room leading onto another and they found themselves led into a sunny room at the back looking out onto a long, narrow garden. It was an interesting room, with lots of influences from their Asian background.

Soon, they were chatting like old friends. Netta was bubbly and pleasant.

"Sam, your room is the one above this. I've pushed the twin beds together. By the way, did you show your bedroom to the parents? Brave man! Rav suggested we might walk up into town to meet him before he closes up. He wants you to see his shop. He is so proud of it. We could have a drink by the river and come back for one of Rav's curries. He more or less made it last night."

To Ella, she said, "You've never had a curry like Rav's, believe me."

Later, they strolled over the wide, busy bridge and into the High Street that bisected the town, as it ran steeply up hill and under a clock set in a high archway. About a third of the way up, Netta stopped and said, "Well, here we are."

The building had a few low windows and a great overhanging first floor. The front was supported on ancient plain stone pillars. They stepped in and found themselves in a modern Pharmacy set in the old Apothecary shop. It was fascinating. Before they had a chance to look about them a tall grey beaded man came out from the small glazed display and shouted with joy when he saw them.

Ella thought *What a happy man,* as he hugged her and Sam and kissed his wife.

"I'm just about to shut up," he said, "but do have a look around." So they did.

It was an incredible mix of gleaming structured steel and wattle and daub walls, which had been left on view in places. Sam hadn't seen it as Ram had been working for a larger chemist when Sam had last been visiting.

"It's great, Rav. How much help do you have?"

"One locum for two days a week and two girls in to cover all day. You've just missed them."

He locked up securely and then slipped his arm through Ella's.

"Now, tell me about yourself." as the set off down the hill.

They were right about the curry. It was to die for and they washed it down with root beer and had a very cordial evening.

"You must come when you can stay," Rav told them when they left the next morning. It was breezy, but mild and the car was open.

Ella waved and shouted, "We will, we will."

"What a wonderful pair," she told Sam. "Did they choose not to have a family?"

"Oh no, it was their dearest wish when they married, but then Netta had three miscarriages, followed by an ectopic pregnancy that almost killed her, so they had to give up. They tried hard to adopt, without any luck. In our culture, people don't give babies up for adoption, the wider family takes care of them and Netta and Rav came up against a general unease about mixed race families. So they have just made the best of what they have, which is a lot."

This sent Ella on a track she had never discussed with him.

"Were you ever discriminated against?" she asked.

"Very little. It helped that we were at private school, with kids from intelligent backgrounds."

"Oooh, get you," she teased him, "but I know what you mean. It is so hateful. I'd never thought about it before, but our children will be mixed race, I suppose."

"So, we're having children are we?" he teased her back. "Thanks for letting me know. Do we need to practise more often?" as he put his left hand on her thigh.

"OK, do behave. Of course I want your children, but not yet." and on they sped towards Cornwall.

St Ives delighted them. Their hotel was close to the centre and their room had a panoramic view of the bay and the harbour. Within a few minutes, they had walked down the hill and settled, with fish and chips in the shelter of the steel wall of the cafe terrace. The sea was turquoise, with little white feathers of waves and, as they studied it, they decided it was on the way in. Sure enough, a small boat that had been lying, forlornly on the wet sand, soon began to bob about on their moorings and, gradually, the music of the lanyards on the masts increased. They could have sat there forever.

Deciding that they couldn't do that, they went off to root around the tiny, cobbled streets, marvelling at the minuscule places the residents managed to stow their cars. It was certainly not built for cars. It was all so very pretty, different from the grandeur of Bath – all white walls and multi-coloured paintwork. There were crocuses in window boxes and daffodils every patch of green there was. They found the Barbara Hepworth garden and spent an hour wandering about, and either admiring or mocking all the statues set out. They could admire the skill and imagination, but they realized they had more traditional tastes in art.

It was late in the afternoon before they strolled back up the hill. The hotel had a very inviting pool in an old orangery, so they changed and went down for a swim. They were alone down their and the light was just dying so the wider water lights were lit and it was very decadent looking, being surrounded by a few large statues in the gardens. Ella discovered Sam was like a fish in the water, a lichenous fish, as it turned out. She was a competent swimmer and they had the most enjoyable hour or so, before emerging to towel themselves and get read to eat. It had been a long day and they decided to have a meal in the hotel and later, much later, they fell asleep in a deep feather bed listening to the distant murmur of the waves.

They spent three days of bliss and really fell in love with St Ives. "I could live here," Sam said one day, as they sat munching pasties on the harbour wall. Ella smiled at him.

"No, seriously, I could. Imagine bringing children up here, with the air blowing straight in off the Atlantic and the freedom of the beaches and the rocks. I don't think I could live right in the middle of the village. It'd be a bit claustrophobic, especially at the height of summer, but imagine a house just outside with views and sound of the sea. I could get a job in the nearest hospital and you could have a gallery. The kids, all four of them, would walk to primary school in the village – there is one, I've seen it. Then they would bus to High School. Speaking of which, Ella, will you marry me?"

Chapter 21

She almost fell off the wall. He grabbed her arm. "Whoa, you can't be that shocked."

"Well, yes, I am, but yes, I will, oh Sam, of course I will," and they fell into a loving clench as the gulls hovered hopefully over the last of the pasties.

When they had recovered their equilibrium, Sam said, "You must have known I wanted you to be my wife."

"Well I suppose I kind of knew, but you've never mentioned marriage, only babies."

"I love you, Ella, more than life itself. I'll love you and take care of you for the rest of my days."

"I know you will, Sam, and I love you more than I can even say."

"Shall we look for a ring now?" Sam was really excited. "Or do you want to wait to shop in Bath?"

"I don't know – give me a chance. I've only been a fiancée for five minutes," but she suddenly said, "I don't want a big flashy diamond. Would you mind if I chose something old?"

"Darling, you can have the Kah-I-Noor if it suits you, but I don't think it would," he laughed. So they drifted off, looking in tiny antique shop windows. Just before the shops closed, they found one in a tiny square. There was some good jewellery in the window, rather than stuff for holidaymakers. The bell jangled as they bent their heads to enter and a lady came through a door.

"Afternoon," she spoke in a lovely warm Devon accent. "Are you looking for something or just browsing?"

She had dark hair, greying on her temples and wore it in a thick plait over one shoulder. Her fingers were covered in rings and her dress was flowing and colourful.

"Everything you see her is either old, or has been remodelled from something old. I like stuff that has a bit of history," she smiled again.

"Well," Ella hesitated, but Sam spoke for her.

"We've just decided to get married." he grinned.

The lady clapped her hands together and her bracelets jingled.

"Oh, how marvellous, and are you looking for a ring, my beauty?"

Ella blushed. "Well, yes. I'd like an older piece of jewellery, but one I can wear all the time."

"In which case, you need a gold setting, so I'll eliminate all the ones that aren't. Gold just improves with being worn. It will gradually wear down, but it should last until you are a great-great-grandmother at least," at which they all laughed.

She turned and opened two drawers.

"I keep these safe," she said, as she lifted the black felt covers.

They were both black velvet liners, filled with rings, set out in grooves.

"Keep away from opals if you want to wear your ring all the time. They're very beautiful, but not tough enough. That's why people think they're unlucky. They're not bad luck as such, but they do chip easily."

So Ella moved her fingers away from an opal that had caught her eye. Then she saw it right away she knew.

"Oh Sam, look at this," as she pointed to a ring set with a heart-shaped emerald with diamond shoulders.

She lifted it and handed it to the lady who said, "Well chosen, now that is a beautiful little ring. The emerald was the centre piece of a Victorian pendant and it was reset on this band about eighty years ago. The gold is 18 carat, which will wear well and the six diamonds are pure whites. Try it on."

Ella did so, on her wedding finger, and it just about slipped on over her knuckle.

"It's perfect, Sam, really perfect," and she went to wriggle it back off her hand, but Sam lifted her hand to his lips and kissed it. His brown eyes looked deep into hers.

"We'll leave it there, then, Ella. It means you're truly promised," at which Ella felt tears well up in her eyes.

The shopkeeper came around from behind the counter and threw her arms around them both.

"Oh," she said, "Oh, this has never happened to me before. Oh, I just knew you two are made for each other. I'm just shutting up.

Come behind and have a drink with me."

And she lead them through the small door into a hippy heaven.

"Mead," she said. "Mead for love," as she drew a golden bottle from a cupboard.

"And my best glasses," as she handed them tall stemmed glasses, rimmed in gilt.

"18th century, these are," she spoke as she poured in the golden liquid.

"To your future."

"To our future."

The room fizzed with their exuberance.

I shall never, ever forget this day, thought Ella.

Sam drew the lady, they never did know her name, to one side and Ella looked around the room. It was cluttered but joyful, with crystals and joss sticks and mild-hued drapes. She realized Sam was discussing paying for the ring.

I never even asked the price, she thought guiltily. *Aren't I a lucky, lucky girl?*

They wandered, arm in arm, back to the harbour, where a small crowd had gathered.

"It's Lifeboat practise tonight," a middle-aged man told them, as they joined the medley.

So they leaned on the railings and watched all the excitement. "I'd love to be involved in all that," Ella suddenly said. "It's so worthwhile, but so thrilling, too. I bet the adrenalin fires off to stop you being scared."

"Well, perhaps when we live here I'll let you, while I babysit the kids," he squeezed her and they laughed.

Neither of them wanted this day to end, and Ella kept having a lingering look at her ring. It glittered as it caught the light and was so very pretty, not at all ostentatious. She just loved it.

It was their last night and they ate a splendid meal at the hotel. She tried not to keep looking at her finger, but felt the waitress had noticed, because she caught her eye and smiled as the wine waiter popped open the bubbly.

On the drive home, they decided they would each let their parents know. She could see problems, but he was quite confident his family would be delighted. They thought they would have a small ceremony in about a year, because Sam would need to give plenty of notice to take a long holiday and he was already thinking of the Seychelles or the Maldives. May next year would be good.

"Just good friends and family, but somewhere really very special, Ella. How does that sound?"

"Perfect. Myra isn't having a huge do. They feel the same way. When we get home we can start to look at our options."

Chapter 22

Once home they rang Joel, their mutual best friend.   He was delighted and next day a huge bouquet of white lilies and a bottle of good champagne arrived.   Good old Joel.

The next evening, Ella spoke to her mother.   She seemed quite pleased, no over the top ever from Annie.

"I suppose we should meet this young man," she said.   Ella noticed the 'we'.

"By the way, I'll give you my new number and address while you're on.   I'm moving in with Charles.   He has a very nice ground floor flat and it makes sense."

"Oh, right," Ella was totally taken aback.   "Are you sure, Ma?"

"Yes, quite sure.   Charles looks after me very well.   Now, should we meet you somewhere half-way for lunch?   You decide and let me know.   We can fit in more easily than you, as Charles has cut down to half weeks and I do the same.   Glad about your news, bye."

Sam told her his parents were very happy about the news and a few days later a large square envelope arrived.   Inside was a very elegant congratulations card and a very generous cheque.

"We'll put that in the honeymoon pot," Sam grinned.   They put off meeting Ma and Charles for a while, as they had a weekend in Penrith soon, for Myra and Andrew's wedding.

The week before they drove up, Sam said he wanted to ask her something serious, something she would need to think about.

She instantly went into panic mode.   "What is it, Sam?   Ask me now, right now."

"OK, OK," he hesitated.   "Ella, could we have a dog?"

Her panic subsided and she laughed.   "A dog, why on earth would we want a dog?"

He shrugged.   "Well, I had a dog I loved when I was at home and he died soon after I went to uni.   I always knew I would have another, but it was something for the future, when I had a house and a garden, but now there's a dog I know needs a home."

"Which dog you know?"

"Ben and his wife, from Ophthalmics are going on a three year VSO in Malawi and they have a rescue greyhound. They can't take him, but they are really upset at the thought of putting him back with the RSPCA. He's about seven they think and he raced for about his first four years. He's very quiet, very clean. He needs a good run once a day, but I'd do all that. I'd see to his food and everything and he's used to being on his own all day. We could put his bed in the kitchen." and he looked at her with his big brown eyes.

"You have this all worked out, haven't you?"

She was surprised at how eager he was. Would they cope two floors up with a dog?

"In three weeks' or so. Shall I bring him to show you?"

"Yes, give me a chance to think about it. What is he called?"

"Bones," he grinned. "Officially he is called Napoleon, but he answers to Bones."

Two days later, he said, "What if Ben brings the dog to see you tomorrow in the lunch hour? I can't get out, I've got clinics."

"OK. Tell him to come to the side door about 12:30 and ring the bell."

Sure enough, the bell rang and she went to open it. She had met Ben a couple of times and they said, "Hi." By Ben's side was one of the most miserable-looking dogs she had ever seen. He saw her expression.

"He's no oil painting, and he's not been well-treated, but he's got a lovely gentle temperament and he's clean and very quiet." She bent down to have a closer look. His name was perfect because he was skin and bones. You could have put your hand round his middle.

"Should he be that thin?"

"Yes, it's the breeding. He's perfectly healthy and has had all his jabs and he's tagged. The vet reckons he must be about seven, but racing ages them faster."

As they spoke, the dog looked at her with sad greeny-brown speckled eyes. She put her hand out and a long tongue licked it continuously.

Ben said, "He likes you. He doesn't often do that to strangers. What d'you think?"

He was so eager, he was like a puppy himself. Ella was thinking to herself, *Would he spoil our carefree life?* But, berating herself for her selfishness, she made a sudden decision.

"Okay, we'll take him. In about three weeks, Sam said."

"Brilliant. Oh, Ella, what a relief. I'll bring everything you need with him and his Vet's card and things." He gave her a peck on the cheek. "I really can't thank you enough. I know he'll be so loved with you and Sam."

She sent Sam a text message. "We are officially dog owners from 20th inst."

Sam was delighted and it did her good to see the pleasure on his face that evening.

They had a weekend to drive up to Penrith for the wedding and had decided to tell Myra and her family after the wedding was over. They had booked Friday and Saturday in a small B&B in the village and arrived quite late, having had a stop on the way up. Sam had never been further north than Liverpool, to meet Joel's family, and he was enthralled by the magnificence of the scenery. Covering the green on the square was a large marquee, all set up for the wedding feast.

They walked to the small church and began to bump into Myra's family. Mike was there, on his own, looking good in grey tails and Cara arrived, alone, in an elegant cream car of ancient vintage. She looked very elegant in a long strapless ivory dress with a small bunch of freesias and a flowered comb in her chignon.

They sat near the back of the small church and enjoyed the soothing organ music. Ella had chosen to wear an emerald green floaty knee-length dress, with a green feather clip in her hair and high heels. Sam looked good in a pale grey suit and they made a very attractive pair. With heels on, Ella was slightly taller than Sam and much taller than most of the other families in church.

Then the vicar walked down to the doors and, to a great burst of sound Myra entered, on her father's arm. She wore a heavy circlet of flowers with a creamy veil over her face. Her dress was like her, unadorned but lovely. It had long, narrow sleeves and a sweetheart neck. The waist was dropped, which made Myra look taller, and the skirt fell into heavy folds, Ella guessed it was silk. The only adornment was a single row of tiny pearls around the neck and down the sleeves. In her ears she had tine pearl earrings and she carried freesias tied with a thick cream ribbon. Ella felt tears well up in her eyes. Myra looked so young and so pure and so radiant. Ella found herself wishing with all her being that she would find true happiness in her marriage to Andrew. Who would walk her down any aisle? She dabbed her eyes and picked up the hymn book.

Afterwards, in the gathering outside church she and Sam managed to congratulate the newly-weds.

"So, this is the famous Sam," Myra was brimming with joy that Sam, unusually quite reserved, held her face lightly in his hands and kissed her gently.

"You are very beautiful, Myra, and I wish you all the luck in the world."

Ella squeezed his hand as they moved away and realized that he, too, was quite emotional.

While the laudau circled the square a few times, amongst waves and laughter, the guests walked to the marquee, which was decorated with small vases of freesias and rich cream roses.

It was a magical day. The family welcomed Sam with such warmth and were delighted to see Ella again, that they really felt very much part of it all. There were speeches, both touching and hilarious, good food and lots of dancing.

By the time Myra and Andrew had departed to a mystery location, Ella and Sam were ready for bed. When they went to thank Myra's parents, Janice said, "Now, you two, we haven't had much of a chance to talk. We're laying on brunch tomorrow. Can you manage that?"

The next morning, they turned up at the Rieds' at about 11 o'clock, having just had coffee at the B&B. The lady had insisted on knocking the price of breakfast off the bill and Sam was amazed.

The Rieds' front door stood open and, as they hesitated, Mike appeared.

"Come on, make yourselves at home. Food is being served out in the garden," and he ushered them through.

It was a fine early summer's day, just warm enough and there was a mini marquee containing a long table. There were all sorts of delicious breakfast dishes, kedgeree and kidneys as well as the more usual bacon etc. It was all being seen to by caterers and, when they had filled their plates and found a small table, Mike came over to perch.

"How's things with you?" he asked, and Ella flashed her hand at him.

"Oh, great, well done, congratulations," he shook Sam's hand and kissed Ella.

"When did this happen?"

"Just a couple of weeks ago. We're going to get married late spring. I don't see Mary about...?" and she left the question in the air.

Mike pulled a rueful face. "No, not any longer. It hasn't been easy. She was just too needy and wanted me by her side all the time. I need more space than that, as you know."

He jumped up. "I'd better circulate and see if they want me for anything."

He'd no sooner gone than his mother arrived. "Oh, it's good to see you, Ella, and looking so well and happy. Myra has told us about you, Sam, and I hope we will get to know you better. You're in medicine, aren't you? Ella, you sly one, is that an engagement ring? Show me. Oh, how lovely, and it suits you so much. Is there another wedding soon?"

John came over to join them and they all had a coffee together before Sam and Ella had to leave, promising to keep in touch.

Chapter 23

The long drive home was full of happy chatter about the day and the sublime little village and the welcoming family.

"Somehow, I don't think Cara is the marrying kind," Sam said at one point.

"What do you mean?" Ella was curious.

"I just have a feeling, time will tell." and they talked about something else.

Ella decided to get a bit more clued up about dogs. She had never had a pet of any description, and she felt she had a duty to find out how to act with Bones when he arrived shortly. She took a book out of the library and studied it. There was a lot of fascinating information there. She had never known that dogs are so intuitive and pick up on owners' moods. Also, she found that they mostly had one real 'head of the pack' figure, but also a lot of time for the person who fed them regularly, so she decided that she would get involved. If they were going to live together, she wanted to be friends with this funny dog. Greyhounds could have quite a hard life if they had been raced. You knew by looking for a tattoo in their ear. Unscrupulous dealers weren't beyond snipping a bit off an ear to disguise their past, because racing had an effect on their life span.

By the time Bones arrived, complete with bowls and basket, leads and a bag of food, she felt more confident about it all.

For a day or two he was unsettled and did a bit of whimpering and wandering around, but she dished up a small bowl of food when she got up and Sam took him out for five minutes. Then they left him in the kitchen with his bed and a small bowl of water. He seemed glad to see whoever returned first and this time had a slightly larger meal, although they had been told he didn't eat a lot. Before they ate, Sam changed into running gear and he and Bones went off for a run, Sam returning hot and sweating for a quick shower. The dog sat with them after that and it wasn't long before he settled. He particularly liked to lie out on the small balcony and, while it was warm enough, the window was left open all evening anyway.

They gave him the odd little tit bit, but she warned Sam not to give him any chocolate. "I've read about it, it poisons dogs," she told him.

One Sunday they met up, for lunch, with ma and Charles at a roadside place somewhere about halfway.

She and Sam were there first, and waited around in the hallway. As her mother walked in, holding Charles' arm, Sam stepped forward, hand outstretched.

"Mrs Hodson, how nice to meet you. I'm Sam Patel."

Her mother just about held the tips of his fingers. "How do you do?" she said in a very formal voice.

Charles shook his hand and hugged Ella. "Good news, I hear." in his cheerful way and her mother guided her to the cloakrooms.

"You never said he was foreign," she snapped as soon as they were alone, "foreign and coloured to boot, I expect he's not even a Christian."

The unfairness of years welled up in Ella. "He's kind and generous and he happens to be one of the youngest cancer specialists in the country. He's a wonderful man, Ma, and I don't go to church now anyway, so we'll go to Hell together. Stuff your Christianity." The outburst obviously shocked her mother.

"There's no need to speak like that, madam."

"Oh yes, there is. I love Sam and he loves me. You have never known what loving was about. As if the colour of his skin makes the slightest difference." and she opened the door and walked out. Her mother was not far behind her.

When they entered the dining area, Charles and Sam were at a table, deep in conversation and both smiled when they saw them.

"Now, tell us your plans," Charles asked, and Annie was forced to join in.

She asked some searching questions of Sam, who glanced once or twice at Ella. He could see she was upset about something.

"And where were you born?" asked Annie.

"In London, and so was my sister."

That seemed to shut her up for a while.

Ella struggled to be civil to her mother, but Charles and Sam, between them, filled in the awkward silences. It was a relief to finish lunch and be able to leave. Sam cited their rush to get back to let their dog out and right away Charles was asking questions.

What a decent man he is, Ella thought. *What does he see in my mother? But then, what had Da fallen for all those years ago?*

In the car, Sam said, "Do I gather your mother wasn't too happy about the news?"

"My mother is never happy about anything," was all she said and he left her, for a while, with her thoughts.

Chapter 24

Bones was such a well-behaved dog that they could take him anywhere. One evening, they all went on the Bizarre Bath Comedy Walk, which lasted about 90 minutes and then they sat outside a pub and fed Bones bits of their steak pies. The weather, while not being brilliant, stayed mild into October and one of the walks they loved to do together was along the Kennet and Avon Canal. They saw friends sometimes, but mostly they just revelled in each others' company, sometimes just two and sometimes three.

The year they had together had just flown. They had begun to look at wedding venues and had more or less settled on a hotel, about ten miles out of the city, where they would have a civil ceremony and a meal on a mid-week day, sometime just ahead of the big Jazz Festival, at the end of May. Although they had enjoyed some of the jazz this year, it did turn into a bit of a gridlock and everywhere was overcrowded. Next year, they would be in the Maldives, they'd settled on that, having read all about the tiny island and the seclusion and luxury.

Unexpectedly, a letter came from Ma. She actually said she had been rather intolerant and that Charles had not been comfortable with her attitude and had asked her to write. Sam did seem a well brought up young man and she would make a big effort to conceal her misgivings. She wished them both well. It was better than nothing, Ella supposed.

Out of the blue, Da rang.

"How are you doing, my Ella, and who's this bloke you plan to marry?"

She told him all her news. "Da, would you give me away?" she suddenly found herself asking. "May, it'll be mid-week in the middle of May. We haven't settled the date yet. It won't be a church do.

There was a silence. "I don't know if I've earned that, Ella. I've not been much of a father to you."

"Da, you were great when I was younger. I would love it if you could."

"Can I think about it?" he asked. "It'd be a posh do, won't it, with him a doctor and all."

"Oh, Da, it will be my wedding. Do try, please."

"I'll let you know well before the day," was all he would commit, but perhaps he would. She had really felt it when Myra's father had walked her into church.

As Autumn changed to Winter, there were almost imperceptible little changes in Sam. She tried to ignore them, but they did begin to bother her. He was thinner. He'd never carried any weight, but now he looked thinner and sometimes he had shadows under his eyes. Although she was, by now, a good cook, and did his favourite food, he wasn't as hungry as he had been. He said he was fine, just tired. When he came in at night, after his run with Bones, he sometimes looked very drawn and they made love less often. One night, when they were having sex, she rolled onto him and he winced.

"What's wrong?" she immediately asked.

"I'm a bit tender just there," he said, cupping his hands behind his waist. "I must have pulled something."

Looking back, they should have done something faster, but doctors are notoriously bad at their own health, as they are constantly fighting to avoid being hypochondriacs.

After that night in bed, Ella made him promise to have a good overhaul.

A few evenings later, as they finished supper, he said, "Ella, we have to talk."

She went cold. Had he changed his mind about her? She couldn't bear it if he had.

Trying to sound calm, she said, "Rightyho. I'm listening." and sat beside him on the sofa.

"I'm not very well, Ella." she opened her mouth, but shut it at the look in his eyes.

"I have a tumour. It's between my liver and pancreas and is nasty. I've had all the scans and I need therapy."

She thought her heart had stopped. "A tumour, what do you mean?"

"It's cancer, Ella," he grabbed her hands tightly. "I have to have treatment soon – early next week."

There was a very long and terrible silence.

He pulled her onto his shoulder. "I'm sorry, I'm so sorry." and she felt his tears running into her hair.

"Sam," she sat up, "darling, you have nothing to apologise for. Come here, let me dry your tears. We'll see this through together. Oh sweetheart, I love you so much, you'll be alright."

"Yes, I will, I know I will I'm fit and young and positive, but there's something else. It's weird, I've advised other blokes who've been patients, but when it comes to yourself..." and he fought to contain himself. "The radiotherapy might make me infertile and I may need chemo as well. If we're to have babies, we have to make a big decision now, tonight really. I can have some sperm frozen and we can use it later on, when I'm well again. It isn't what we would want, but would it be better than nothing?"

Oh dear God, Ella fought hard. "What exactly would it mean, Sam?"

"Well, I'd have to provide some sperm and it would be sent to Long Term Sperm Storage, probably in Manchester. There are only a few hospitals with the facilities and that's the big one. They can store it for over 50 years." he tried to laugh. "We won't need that long. It should work because I'm young. It has a good success rate. Then, when we're ready we have a few options, but we can leave that for later."

"What would you have to do?" at this he grinned feebly.

"Just lock myself in somewhere with a porn magazine. What's not to like?" An even larger silence.

"And if you don't?"

"Probably no little Patels."

"What do you want to do?"

"I want our babies and if this is what it's going to take, I'll get on with it, but are you sure, Ella?"

"I want your babies, Sam. If it doesn't upset you – do you want me to come with you?"

"No, not tomorrow, but you can come with me when I start radiotherapy next week – just the first time, when I see the consultants."

"Of course I will. I'll come all the time. What happens, how often do you have to go and how long for? What does it do?" She was suddenly full of questions.

"I'm tired, sweetie, wrung out, let's go to bed and talk in the morning," and that's what they did.

She lay still, with her head spinning and tried hard not to give in to her panic. She must be strung she must.

After a while she knew Sam was asleep. Her eyes never closed all night long. She felt every move he made and listened to his breathing, willing it all to have been a nightmare, hoping to suddenly wake from it all, yet knowing it was real. She had to control this feeling of dread. She had to be his support. In the end, she fell back on the prayer of her childhood, "Hail Mary, full of grace," over and over in her head. She prayed Sam would soon be better, that the treatment wouldn't be too awful and that she could be strong.

Chapter 25

Over breakfast, she had more questions. Why couldn't he have an operation? What exactly was radiotherapy? He gave her all the answers, patiently and quietly. Then she said, because she couldn't help her thoughts, "But why you, Sam? You're so young and fit, why you?"

"Because cancer doesn't have much logic, Ella. It hits all sorts of people, lots of people who deserve it much less than I do. I've got you to battle it with me, the whole of the Oncology department right there with me and no money worries. I sometimes see patients with a mortgage and children, terrified of how they are going to manage while they have a lot of time off work. If this bloody illness does nothing else, it will help me to understand more what my patients are going through."

He reached across the table and grabbed her hand.

"We must be positive about this Ella. It's the only way."

When he came in from the hospital the next evening, he put his arms round her and spoke against her cheek.

"Well, that's done, Ella. We'll forget it now until I'm better. I start radio on Monday – six weeks every weekday. When the tumour has shrunk, they'll give me a month or two before they start chemo. That should do the trick." He spoke very convincingly and Ella fought to feel the same confidence.

She had never known much about cancer and she had a lot to learn. Sam had never spoken much about his job and she had always sensed he chose to leave it behind him, when he wasn't at the hospital.

The only concession Sam asked, and was given, was that he had his treatment early every day, so that he could get straight back to his vocation. Ella told Mr and Mrs Asquith about it and, after their initial shock and horror, they were a tower of strength. She went with him to Radiology in the mornings and then straight to her job at the Museum. The treatment seemed very simple. Sam only spent about fifteen minutes shut away and it didn't initially seem to be having much effect on his life.

They became used to the routine and everyone was so kind and efficient. Inevitably, Sam bumped into a few of his patients, having the same treatment and they were all so very supportive and cheerful that Ella found herself relaxing a little. Other people seemed to cope so well and so must she. Christmas and New Year came and went, very quietly.

By then, Sam was feeling a bit tired and couldn't eat a big meal. Some evenings, Ella took Bones out for his walk, but, most of the time, life carried on fairly normally.

She gave Sam a soft calf skin holdall for Christmas, when she noticed the condition of the bag he had had for ever and he surprised her with a tiny emerald on a fine gold chain, so beautiful against her creamy neck.

Their sex life had quietened down, but they constantly cuddled and kissed and were closer than ever. Sam had small tattoo marks on his skin, to mark where they had to hit with the radiation and Ella would be kissing them, while he stroked her hair. He reckoned he was lucky, because his darker skin didn't burn, as some people did from the treatment. He never complained.

He had written to his parents, trying to explain it to them gently and they rang every few days to ask how he was. He put them off coming to visit.

"When I've finished with all this and I can enjoy a meal with you again. Come then, in the spring," she had heard him tell them one evening.

The plans for the wedding went on hold. There was no rush. They could get married any time, when Sam was better.

The radiotherapy seemed to do what it should and the tumour had shrunk, although not as much as they might have hoped and it was decided that the chemo was to be sooner rather than later. He joked about losing his hair, if he did lose it.

"You won't really notice," he smiled at her because he always had his hair cropped very short. In the event, he didn't seem to lose any.

But he was losing weight. He tried very hard to eat more fattening foods, but he wasn't digesting fats well and they just made him sick. He knew how to treat himself and drank a fortified vitamin drink every morning, which he hated.

They sometimes had a stroll together with Bones, but more often now Ella took him for a walk, or a run, on her own while Sam lay listening to music. Joel called on them a lot and they were always glad to see him. Sometimes he had a meal with them, mostly pasta or salads, which Sam enjoyed. Without speaking about it too much, Joel's very presence reassured them both.

The chemo hit Sam hard. They went one day a week where he was hooked up for an hour. She drove because he always felt groggy afterwards. Then he would seem to recover and be more himself for a few days before it was all repeated, but more and more often he would be very sick and began to spend a lot of time rushing to the bathroom. He wasn't well enough for his taxing job and his colleagues made him take some sick leave.

He didn't argue the point, as he would have done a few months ago. She asked if she could cut her hours for a while and the Asquiths said she must.

Life fell into a different pattern. She let Bones out in the morning and made a light breakfast for her and Sam. Then she went off for the morning, while Sam came to slowly and was showered and dressed when she got in about 1pm. Some days they had a little walk, or a short explore in the car, but more and more they sat reading, or listening to music, and sometimes they watched TV.

The apartment had such a great view and was always so full of light that they never felt confined and Ella bought a couple of bird feeders and they took great delight at watching the variety of birds that appeared for the seeds and nuts. They even bought a book so they could identify them.

They waited, as patiently as they could, for this awful treatment to be finished and rejoiced when it was. So the news, when they were told, was a hammer blow. Far from being destroyed, the tumour had grown and the scan now showed secondaries. There was nothing more they could do. The senior doctor who told them this had tears in his eyes.

"I feel so helpless, Sam, and so dreadful. We hoped it might work, but you knew it was a bad one."

"Yes, I know."

Sam stood up from his chair and patted the older man on the shoulder.

"You did your best. It wasn't to be. Thank you."

Ella just sat, unbelieving. What were they saying? They couldn't mean Sam was going to die. She heard a strange keening sound and Sam was beside her.

"Don't, Ella, don't cry. I've known for a while now. We'll be alright."

A nurse appeared with two mugs of sweet tea. She was trying hard to be professional, but wasn't managing too well.

"Oh, Sam, I'm sorry. I'm so sorry," and she squeezed both their shoulders. "Just stay here as long as you want," and she left them alone.

Ella sat in Sam's arms and cried until she could cry no more. This couldn't be happening. Sam couldn't die.

Gradually, her sobs subsided. Sam handed her a handful of tissues.

"Shall we go home now?" and hand in hand they made their slow way out of the clinic Sam had loved so much.

Ella didn't, couldn't turn up for work the next day. They were both shattered and quiet. She rang the Museum and asked for a couple of days off. She didn't want to let them down; Joel came the second day and cried with them.

But you can't cry forever, she found. Bones needed to be fed and walked and Sam needed nourishment too. She had to drag herself towards a bit of normality. Somehow, she found the willpower.

A few nights later, when they were cuddled together on the sofa, Sam said, "There's something I've thought about these last few weeks, but I think it might be a big ask," he hesitated. "I don't want a grave, or a cremation, Ella."

She groaned as she put her head on his chest.

"Don't, Sam, I just can't bear it, don't, please."

"But we must, sweetheart. I'm not going to be here for a lot longer. I know I won't and we have to talk about things. Just listen to me, please just listen."

So she made a huge effort and lay still as he talked. He wanted her to agree to him giving his body to the hospital. His was an unusual cancer to hit a young man and the therapy hadn't done it. Why? Perhaps from him they could find out more about it and how to conquer it. Perhaps it could help others in the future.

"And there's another reason, too. I don't want you to spend the rest of your life tending a grave, and tied to somewhere I've been. I want you to live a life, Ella. You're very young and have so much to give. Tell me you'll carry on and make a good life after I've gone. I couldn't bear to think of you tied to somewhere because of me," his voice broke and he gave in to his tears and fears. "Will you do that for me, darling Ella? Can I know you'll be free?"

She lay trying to assimilate what he had said. She just wished they could turn the clock back a year. She didn't feel she could cope with it all, but she knew she would do anything under the sun that would ease his agony.

After a while, she asked him, in a low voice, "So what would happen when..." and she trailed off, she couldn't say it, "when you die," her mouth wouldn't say the words.

He picked up on it, as he always understood her so well.

"I'd arrange it all with Joel. He could take over. He'll see you're alright and sort things out.

"Have you spoken to him?"

"Not yet, but I want to, if you agree."

"Yes, Sam, if that will make you happy. I'd do anything to make you happy."

"Right, I'll meet you with Joel tomorrow. I'll give him a ring to see if he's free anytime."

Joel came the next evening and Ella left them alone while she took Bones out.

Chapter 26

As she was opening the front door, Mr Green, who lived on the first floor, was coming out. They were on pleasant terms, but no more than that. She'd never had a conversation with him. He was in his early sixties she thought, with a mop of iron grey hair. He smiled at her, then hesitated.

"Could I have a word?" he fondled Bones as he spoke. "I really don't want to interfere, but I gather your partner is very ill. Would it help if I gave him a good walk in the evenings? I've owned a few dogs in my time and it would give me some exercise and it would be one less thing for you to worry about."

She nearly threw her arms around him.

"What a generous offer. It would be a load of my mind, as I do worry about leaving Sam sometimes."

So it was arranged. Mr Green came up and rang the bell at about the same time every evening and kept Bones out for a good half hour, or more if it was a fine night.

People are so kind, Ella thought. *We don't even really know him.* In fact, they knew few people, apart from those they both knew. They hadn't needed other company, but people were good.

Sam's position was being filled temporarily, although they all knew what the outcome was going to be, but they pretended he was going to get his health back. Meanwhile, he was on his full salary.

He had made sure she understood his financial position. Any savings he had he had already transferred to her account and it was a considerable amount. He would be insured through the NHS and she would get a lump sum and he also had a large life insurance package. He had made certain all this would be paid to her, as his next of kin.

"At least you won't have money worries, darling. That's one thing I can do for you."

Sam's colleagues took to popping in to keep him in the loop. They had the sense to make them short visits but, even then, he was exhausted when they had gone. Then he started with a dull ache in his back, that grew worse. Ella spoke to Joel and he passed it on and they had a call one day from two nurses from the local Hospice. They were brilliant, just matter of fact, whilst kind. They offered Sam pain relief and asked him if he would like to self-administer, as he was much better qualified than they were and somehow they all managed to smile at this.

They would call on Tuesdays and Fridays, to keep an eye on things, unless Ella needed help, in which case she was to just call them.

Sam was visibly going downhill. His voice had weakened and he was dreadfully thin. The nausea was with him most of the time and he spent more and more time sleeping.

Ella pushed the black chair into the bedroom and sat there while he slept. She didn't want to waste a second of their time away from him.

Joel brought food with him, and sat and watched her eat, as she had lost a lot of weight herself. He told her she had to keep healthy and she knew he spoke sense.

The nurses provided a special gel mattress cover for their bed, to ensure Sam's comfort and Ella coped. She prayed whenever she felt about to panic and it seemed to help. She knew now there were no miracles coming, but she prayed that he wouldn't suffer much more and she prayed that she could keep calm. He didn't need panic around him in his last weeks on earth.

She achieved all this. The flat sparkled and had an air of peace. Sam's music was on low most of the time and she sat by him and watched him and sometimes she read to him.

One April evening, the light of a full moon illuminated the apartment and she helped Sam to the big armchair.

"How beautiful it all is, almost as beautiful as you, my sweetheart."

They stood for a short while before walking gently back to the bed.

She lay that night holding his hand as they talked of the things lovers talk. Then Sam dozed off and after a while she began to relax and she slept also.

In the morning, only one of them woke.

Chapter 27

It all became a blur for Ella. There were bits she recalled. Joel arriving. Mr Green taking her down to his place and making her drink brandy. Going to sleep in Joel's bed and kind people in and out of Joel's bedsit. But most of it was just a grey nothingness. She wanted to die, to go where Sam had gone. Why had he gone, where was he? She didn't cry, she was too empty to cry. She didn't shower or wash her hair. She didn't want to be alive so why should she bother about being clean?

There was no conception of time. Mostly she slept. Joel made her force food down sometimes and she almost choked on it. *Why don't the just let me die?* she wondered.

But slowly, she began to come back to life. Life was dreadful, but she was here and had to get on with it. Joel was incredible and one day she realized how much he must be suffering and how thoughtless she had been. That shook her. Joel had been Sam's friend for years before she met them and she had ignored his anguish. That evening, she had a shower and told Joel she would go back to the flat. She looked at him for the first time, properly, and saw how drawn and pale he was.

"I'm sorry, Joel," she patted his hand. "I've been so miserable I've never thought about you. I'm truly sorry," and she reached her arm around his big shoulders and he gave in and cried in her arms.

The next day he took her home. The hallway was jammed with cards and letters. Joel picked them up and put them on the table.

"Are you alright?" She knew he was concerned about leaving her. "Promise me you'll be sensible."

"Yes, Joel, I will. I made a promise to Sam and I've got to keep it. I'll be alright, honestly I will."

Of course, she was anything but alright, but she made herself go through the motions. She ate a little and she drank a little and she even had coffee with Mr Green, who brought Bones back. Apparently he had whisked him away.

She realized that she had never given a thought to where the dog was and she felt ashamed.

A couple of days later, Joel asked, "Do you think we should arrange some sort of little service to remember Sam?"

She thought about it. "We aren't religious at all." she said. She was still in the present tense.

"No. I know that – just a bit of music and a little talk about Sam. People seem to need it and it might be better for you. It would be something definite to do, wouldn't it?"

So it was decided and Joel took over.

She plucked up all her courage and rang Mr and Mrs Patel. In his distress Joel hadn't thought to tell them of Sam's wishes, so it was up to her to explain and this she managed to do. She spoke to Sam's father, who was kindness itself. His wife was still quite unwell, her heart had never been perfect but she seemed a little stronger every day. Ella explained what she and Joel had decided to do and he said he would talk to his wife and call her back shortly.

He rang the next day. "As it's quite a trip for us and my wife is still unwell, we've decided to have our own small memorial, here, with our friends and remember Sam that way. That doesn't upset you, does it, Ella? That would be the last thing we would want."

She told him that she fully understood, and she did. She promised to write soon, when she felt up to it.

She never gave her own mother a thought, not for weeks, anyway.

Joel arranged to have their little service in the chapel at the hospital. It was totally non-denominational, and it was peaceful. It would also be so convenient for those who had worked with Sam and who were on duty.

So, on a spring morning, with Bath full of daffodils, Joel took Ella up to the hospital chapel. She had made a huge effort, for Sam's sake, and wore a grey maxi dress and her hair in a chignon. There were far more people than she had expected. She saw Mr and Mrs Asquith and Sam's past landlady and, of course, lots of people from the hospital. To her surprise, Mr Green came in and sat at the back.

There were white lilies in the ledges and the heady perfume hung in the air. When they had all settled, the sounds of music began to fill the chapel. Ella had chosen Bette Midler singing *Wind Beneath*

My Wings, a favourite of hers and one she used to sing to Sam. Joel sat holding her hand in his. As the music died away, he stood up and went out to the lectern. He spoke about his friend Sam, about his great achievements in his chosen career and his compassion and humour, but mostly he spoke of his great love for Ella and of the joyous time they had together. As he struggled through, his voice almost breaking, Ella sat quietly. She didn't cry, she felt too empty. Joel sat down and she grasped his hand. Then, though she found there were no tears left, as she and those who had known and loved and respected her Sam sat and listened to Leonard Cohen's *Alleluia*, Sam's all time favourite.

When the strains died away, there were few who were not in tears. After a few minutes, Joel pulled her to her feet and they waited for the people to leave by the door.

"That was beautiful."

"Well done, Ella."

"I'm so very sorry."

The voices and the faces passed by. In the end, just Joel remained.

"Thank you, Joel. That was all I could have wished for. Now I've got to try and get on."

They sat talking that afternoon. Ella decided she was going to go back to work the following Monday and she spoke with Mr Asquith, who was delighted.

"The best thing you could do, Ella," he said. "You must try to get on with life. Please God, in time the pain will ease."

She didn't feel as if it would. She was hollow inside and felt as if a grey blanket was over her, weighing her down, so that every little thing was more than she could manage.

She made a huge effort. Her smart clothes came out of the wardrobe, where they had been, untouched, for months and she put some outfits together. She set her alarm and, every weekday, she got up, showered, dressed, had a mug of instant coffee and walked to the Museum. In the lunch break, she, perhaps, had a sandwich, and she did her job. She felt she wasn't really alive, she was just going through the motions and stay sane.

She lost the art of sleep altogether and became more and more weary. In the end, Joel told her she must go to her GP and tell him she scarcely slept, so she did. He was very understanding and said he thought she needed a light sedative, to help her get back into a pattern of sleeping. She learnt to take one mid-evening, which seemed to calm her by bedtime and she was at least having a few hours of proper rest. She also had to make herself eat. She shopped once a week and bought one person freezer meals, which she popped in the microwave every evening. She knew she had to keep plodding on, if only because she didn't want to let Sam down. She just got by in a sort of lethargic nightmare and could see no light at the end of the tunnel. The poor dog was miserable too and she had no way of improving things for either of them.

Then a few things that happened that, at least, dragged her out of her lethargy.

One evening, she had asked Mr Green in for a coffee, having met him on the stairs. He was a thoughtful, quiet man and she liked his company.

Suddenly, he asked, "What are you doing about the car, Ella?" and she just looked at him in confusion. "It's just that it doesn't seem to have moved for a long time and it's going to deteriorate if you don't begin to use it. You do drive, don't you?"

"Yes, oh yes, I can drive. I haven't even thought about it, Mr Green. I just walk or catch the bus. What should I do?"

"Well, I took the liberty of looking and you will need to tax it next month and presumably the insurance will run out at the same time. So you need to get an MOT done before then." He looked at her gently. "Do you want me to help?"

"Oh, would you?" The she suddenly realized that she really would never want to drive Sam's car again.

"Would it be crazy to sell it? I never really enjoyed driving it. I always felt too low down. It was Sam's car, not my choice. What do you think?"

"If you honestly feel like that, I could make you a good offer for it, Ella, and help you find a car you'd feel happier with. Now I've retired I could enjoy a few mad years in a car like that. I'd find out its market value and pay you all its worth. Think about it and let me know," and there it was left.

Chapter 28

The next time she saw Joel, she told him about the chat she had had and he said it sounded a sensible move. He knew she didn't love the low-slung driving position and he was more of a Land Rover man himself. If Mr Green was prepared to buy it and help Ella fund a new car, it would be ideal.

And so the deal was done. The cash from the car went into the bank, joining a great deal of money that was accumulating from private and NHS insurances and Sam's pension pot. They already had a healthy amount before Sam's death and now there was a big sum of money and, one day, she would have to do something about it.

She told Mr Green she wanted a second hand hatch back – just a reliable runabout. They settled on a silver Fiesta, with a low mileage and one lady owner. It only cost a fraction of the money she had from Sam's car, but it suited her needs. It made her smile when she first saw Mr Green wrapping a scarf around his neck and jamming on a leather cap and carefully lowering himself into his new toy. It was going to give him some adventure and she was glad.

The next big thing was a letter from Ma. She didn't often write and Ella tore open the envelope. She suddenly realized she hadn't even told Ma about losing Sam. The letter shook her, even though they had little contact. Charles had found a place on the Dordogne and, now he had fully retired, they were planning to live there full time. They would be moving to France in six weeks and she gave Ella her new address. She assumed she was living with 'that young man' and hoped she would keep in touch. Ella felt strangely deserted, but then she gave herself a mental shake. After all, it took more than one to make a close relationship and she made little contact herself. At last, she made an effort and wrote back and told her mother her tragic news.

Ma rang when she got the letter, and told Ella she was welcome to stay with them when they had settled. She offered her sympathies.

"He was too young to die, Ella."

Yes, thought Ella, *I know.*

Netta rang, she rang almost every week and they were always glad to talk to each other. She was ringing to tell Ella about a five day bereavement course that was going to be at Dartington Hall, close to where they lived.

"It might sound morbid, Ella, but I know a girl who went to a similar course after her husband was killed in Afghanistan and she said it was really wonderful. You could have a few days here before and after and it is a really glorious venue, pastoral and beautiful. Have a think about it and ring me. Don't leave it too long, as the courses at Dartington are usually filled up quickly."

"Right," she told herself. "I've spoken to Ma and I've done something about the car. Maybe this course would be a good idea and it would be good, anyway, to see Rav and Netta."

She went on the Web and found what she was looking for. She could live in full board and have a single room en suite. There were various speakers, one of whom was a famous actress a widow herself and somebody Ella had always admired. That settled it. She booked herself in and paid a deposit before she could change her mind. Netta was delighted.

She suggested Ella go down by train, but Ella had decided she would rather be independent and anyway, it was time her little Fiesta had a proper drive. Joel thought it a great idea and so did Mr Green, who had become Will.

"Leave Bones with me," he immediately offered. Bones liked Will, in fact she often thought he liked him more than he liked her. Will said he was probably more a man's dog. She looked after him well, but he never seemed to be very happy and she would have liked him to be a bit more affectionate.

"He probably misses Sam a lot," she reasoned.

She arranged a week off and drove down on a spring day. The car behaved very well and tackled the last hill with spirit and she actually enjoyed the drive. Netta and Rav hugged her until she was breathless and made her feel very wanted.

They took her uptown the next day, to the market, where she saw a lot of very unorthodox people and weird and wonderful clothes. Totnes was certainly a very alternative sort of town and she loved it all. The local accent was soft and gentle and made it seem like everyone was being particularly welcoming.

The next morning, they all went down river, on the ferry to Dartmouth, where they had lunch and caught the bus back. She could see why they had fallen in love with this area, it wasn't difficult.

That evening, they drove ahead of her to her residence for the next few days and made sure she was safely ensconced. It really was delightful – an ancient collection of buildings around a large-lawned cloister, with gardens spreading as far as the eye could see.

Her room was simple, but pleasant and had a terrific view down over sloping lawns.

There was a welcoming supper mid-evening and she told Rav and Netta she would stay over again next Saturday, if that was alright.

"Just relax and absorb it all," Rav said. "The very atmosphere of the place will help you."

She plucked up courage and went down to the Refectory, to find a mixed bag of people drifting in, mostly in ones and looking a bit unsure, just like her. The seating was at round tables for ten and you could sit anywhere.

Ella sat down at a table with one other lady, a lot older than her and they introduced themselves. Gradually, all the places filled up and a very good meal was served. Over the meal they began to chat about their journey and the surroundings, all very impersonal. There was an adjoining bar, but Ella decided that was a bit much for her and went up to bed quite early. She took her tablet and slept well and couldn't think where she was when she woke. A quick shower soon woke her and she made her way to the first seminar.

Some of the speakers, during the week, were on the purely practical side, discussing finances and assistance and banking etc., but mostly they were people with their own input and some of them were very interesting and thought-provoking. Ella soon found herself making small talk and having an hour in the bar in the evening. The other people gradually began to unwind and some of them discussed their loss and their state of mind. Ella couldn't do that yet. She just knew she would cry, but nobody pushed and asked her probing questions and she became more confident in what she was taking in. One evening, she talked to a middle-aged lady who had lost her husband and son in a car accident. She also had a daughter and a grandchild and told Ella that they were what kept her going.

There were a couple of people about her own age and some who were really old, but all were suffering the pain of loss and that common factor seemed to form a very unlikely bond, so that they began to laugh and chat with each other. They nearly all made use of the gardens and you could find yourself wandering along a path in the company of any of them.

Ella had time to think and reflect and she began to have a half-baked idea. The speaker on the last day made all these ideas seem possible and inspired Ella beyond her wildest dreams. It was as if she suddenly began to feel young life flowing back into her veins again and she hung on her every word.

This was the actress, who had been married to a fellow actor, both well-known on stage and TV. He had died of cancer a few years previously and she spoke of her despair. To add to her agony she had already lost her first husband to cancer as well. As their children had flown the nest they had acquired a second home in Provence, a simple place which they adored, but, when she eventually returned on her own she was most unsettled and unhappy. At first she decided to sell up and forget Provence, but then she took time to consider her options. She realize that it was the familiar house without her Richard that had so unsettled her, not the actual area in which it as. Perhaps she could find some pleasure again in Provence by moving to a different area in a new home. After much soul-searching this was what she had done. She had bought a smaller home, just large enough for some friends of family and chosen just to suit her. With trepidation she had moved in and immediately began to feel at peace there. This was not 'their' home, it was hers.

This hit a note with Ella. The flat had always been Sam's and his choice, no matter how perfect his ideas had been. She didn't feel at home there now that Sam was no longer there. She could sell up and give Sam's parents their money back and buy somewhere smaller. But where? If she was going to move would she still want to live in Bath and keep her job at the Museum, or should she make a really life-changing move?

When the course ended, she drove back to Totnes and talked over her idea with Sam's loving sister and her husband. They advised her to give it some time and not to make any decision too rapidly. Then, if she still felt in the same mode they both suggested that, perhaps, a whole new start would be better for her than being in a place where she was constantly being reminded of the past and what should have been her future.

All the long drive home, the thoughts went on and on through her head. Should she, shouldn't she. Where would she go, what would she do for a job? She seemed to be safe financially for a while, but she would need to buy somewhere – her head was spinning.

The week away had done her good and Bones actually seemed glad to see her, which gladdened her heart. Back at work she tried to settle, but she was just starting to feel life coursing through her veins again and she constantly tossed around, in her head different scenarios.

One morning, she suddenly thought of St Ives. She and Sam had their dreams about Cornwall and they had had such a magical few days there together. But then her common sense kicked in and she realized that St Ives would be full of too many memories and it could prove to be even worse than Bath without Sam. Anyway, where could she work somewhere like that? She also knew she had to get her finances sorted out before she made any huge decisions.

When she confided her daydreams to her two closest friends, Joel and Will, they both gave it serious thought and both, reassuringly, said the same sort of thing. She should sort out her financial position first. Then, when that was done and she felt she had a decent cushion to fall back on, she should go a step further. Basically, they seemed to agree that it might be good for her, but both were reluctant to lose her living close by.

She took her courage in both hands and rang Sam's parents. Some months had gone by and she hoped it was now time to see them and talk to them about the flat. They seemed very pleased to hear from her and delighted when she asked if she could come up to London to see them. She had a couple of personal things of Sam's she wanted to give them, which was as good a reason as any. Instantly, they asked her to stay, but she didn't feel ready for that. Instead, she suggested that she caught the early train and they could have lunch somewhere and then she could get back to Bath in the evening.

"You must come to our home, Ella," said Sam's mother. "Just pop in a taxi – it will take about 15 minutes, dependant on traffic."

So that is what she did. She took Sam's gold cuff links and some framed family photographs and arrived, in late morning, outside an elegant house in Hampstead. The door flew open and Sam's father, looking smaller and older, came out to greet her.

This is how Sam would have looked had he become an old man, she thought, as the wiry arms encircled her shoulders.

His wife was at the door.

"You are so welcome, child," she said as she kissed her.

"Come in, come in," and she lead the way across the parquet hall floor and through double doors into an exquisite drawing room.

"Oh, it's so lovely," Ella breathed as her host plumped up a chair for her.

"It's a Regency house, isn't it?"

They both nodded agreement and Ella sank into a chair and took it all in. There were floor to ceiling bay windows at either end and a view of an elegant garden slightly lower than the window. Sunlight filled the room and there were glorious lamps and artefacts that proudly suggested the origins of the owners. All was creams and golds, but not brash or showy. It filled Ella with delight and she said as much. They were both so happy at her appreciation that it eased the situation.

"We are lifelong collectors, really," they spoke together, "and we did have some family heirlooms."

"Would you like coffee or tea, or perhaps a glass of sherry?"

"Actually, a glass of sherry would go down very well, thank you," and he produced a bottle and glasses from a magnificent armoire.

Ella picked up her bag and removed the little parcels, in tissue paper. As she expected there were a few tears shed as they were opened, but they all pulled themselves together and Mr Patel said, "A toast to our wonderful son," as they sipped at their cool sherry.

"Lunch will be in half an hour," Mrs Patel said. "Would you care to have a little walk in the garden first, Ella?"

"Well, actually, I need to discuss things with you," Ella hastily said. "Could we do that before lunch, please?"

She had to get it over with, or she would fluff it all up.

"Of course, child, whatever will suit you."

So Ella began. She told them of her very vague plan and she had written down the sum in Sam's bank. Mr Patel just glanced at it without comment.

"If I go ahead the flat would be sold and it's your flat. Would you be alright with that? I would just have the money to put into your account on completion," she said.

After she had explained herself there was a short silence and then both the Patels made to speak at once. Mrs Patel waved her hand at her husband as if to say 'you carry on', and he did.

"Ella, my dear Ella, the money in that bank account is yours now. It has nothing to do with us, As for the apartment, yes, we did originally purchase it for our son, but it was gifted to him, with our love and pride. Sam was very happy there and you looked after him and gave him such joy. Now Sam has gone, that apartment is yours to do with whatever you wish. I can quite see that what you are considering is the best solution to help you to move on in your life. If you do take the decision, at least my wife and I will know you will be free from the huge stress of financial hardship and you would have our blessing."

Ella was stunned.

"But..." she began.

He put his brown gnarled hand on her arm.

"No buts, Ella. This is what we want for you. We would only ask that you will always keep us in your heart. You are our only link to our dear boy."

Mrs Patel came across to her and hugged her. "Now shall we go in for lunch?"

They went through to another magnificent room, with French windows and steps to a flagged terrace. The oval table was set up and as they sat a young girl, of about 20, came in with bowls of salad.

"This is Mina," said Mrs Patel, and Mina smiled at Ella. "She is our right hand, now we are slowing down a bit. She is a great girl and a very good cook. I know you like spicy food – Sam told me, so I hope you enjoy this traditional dish."

She took Ella's plate and put a ladle full of aromatic golden casserole to one side.

"See how you like that," she murmured.

It was delicious, just spicy enough to be interesting and Ella had another serving. Then a homemade mango sorbet was produced and enjoyed.

Later, they strolled in the garden. Ella's mind was in a whirl. She tired to convey her appreciation of their huge generosity, but they made light of it. When her taxi came, they each hugged her and made her promise not to lose touch.

"Of course, I shan't. You are both so kind. I was so lucky to meet your gentle, kind son. Goodbye and thank you for everything."

Chapter 29

On the train she sat and mulled over what she now knew. She would be in a very comfortable financial position, with the world before her. This startling new development had served to polarize her position and she realized she really did want to forge a new life for herself.

She did nothing in a rush. It wasn't in her nature. First off, she did a great deal of considering. What did she see as her future life? Where would she, ideally, want to live and in what sort of house? How did she want to earn her living, because she needed to do that, for her own pride? How much did she need company? Most of all, what would Sam be happy with her doing? One huge thing she didn't even dare to put to paper. She had it there, though, in the back of her mind.

I'll give myself time, she thought, *and see what evolves.*

One day, she bought a small tapestry canvas and took up a hobby from her teenage years. It was comforting to sit by the big window, with her threads and artfully draw a picture with her needle. She kept it simple, but was really pleased with the result. There was a lot of sky and sea and a lone seagull perched on an upturned boat, her memories of St Ives again.

She had a long, newsy letter from Myra. She and Andy were to be parents and her letter bubbled with joy. Her brother, Mike, was footloose and fancy free again. Had she heard from Jackie or Joanne?

For the first time in months she felt able to sit down and write to her uni pals and tell them what had happened. It did her good to get it down on paper and accept that what she wrote was fact. Sam would never be back again. She must strike out on her own now.

One lunch hour, she picked up a sandwich and a magazine and sat by the river. A title jumped off the page at her; "The St Ives of the Welsh Coast"

She read it avidly. It was about a coastal village on the Llyn

Peninsula, beloved by artists and full of people making a living by photography, writing, painting etc. There were photographs of whitewashed cottages and houses, a huge expanse of sand and distant mountains. It excited her deeply and she kept getting it out of her bag to have a look at it again. Could this be an answer? Somewhere like St Ives, minus the memories.

When she got back home, she went on the computer and looked up information about the Llyn and found that it was almost on the top corner of Wales, sticking out into a huge bay and not too far from Caernarvon, trains, larger shops, etc. It sat on the Gulf Stream and had its own micro-climate and was an area of natural beauty. It also sounded very arty and ideas began to crystallize. She looked up property and prices – not cheap – but she was now going to be quite comfortably off and the money from the flat would easily cover a simple house.

In the midst of these decisions, Mike rang her. He was going to be in the area. Could they have lunch?

He looked totally unchanged and it was so good to see him. They easily fell into their old companionable ways and she poured her heart out. It was really good to talk to him about Sam and her thoughts. He was footloose and fancy free and on his way to an interview at a prestigious golf club further south. He was enjoying being single and in no rush to find a girlfriend. They talked and talked together and Ella realized how much she enjoyed his company. She knew how lucky she was to have male friends, who had no expectations of any romance, because she didn't think she would ever want to fall in love again, or have sex with anyone else – ever.

He was very supportive of her ideas and the more she discussed it the more realistic it seemed to get.

She decided she would at least go to have a good look at the area and what it offered.

Mike went off for his interview and, within a week or so, she heard from Myra and Joanne. They were both dreadfully upset at her tragic news and expressed their dismay that they were so far away. Their letters were so heartfelt that, even though they made her cry, they also reminded her of the people who cared for her and were so upset on her behalf.

She had to prove worthy of all the support – and she would.

She was so excited that she had a knot in her stomach when she went to keep her appointment with the solicitor in town. He turned out to be a rather severe gentleman, probably in his 60s, who was totally flummoxed when she told him it would be a cash sale.

Had she not a property to sell, he wanted to know and was even more put out when she said she had, but had a buyer lined up ad didn't need to sell before she bought. She felt obliged to explain, at which he softened a little and offered sympathy on her loss.

She told him she would be heading back to Bath to tie things up at her end and he shook hands and promised to do all he could to facilitate a quick settlement. He also suggested she might like to keep in touch to help her in any other business and she thought perhaps she would. After all, it would save explaining her situation again.

It was a fine day and the drive was easier, because she was in an upbeat mood, but she stopped to have a snack at the pub in Welshpool. The same girl, Jenny, was on duty and she felt she had to tell somebody, so it all spilled out and Jenny seemed genuinely pleased for her.

"Do let me know how you get on. I think you are really courageous," she said, and Ella promised she would.

A good run back and she went downstairs to tell Will all about it, over a glass of his favourite red wine.

"I shall miss you, Ella," he said. "Both you and Bones, but you are doing the right thing, that I am sure. Do keep in touch. I shall never forget you and Sam and the dog."

He sounded quite sad, but then grinned. "And of course I am so much enjoying the crazy car. It makes me feel like a young man again."

Ella rang Joel and told him her news. His reaction was shock that it had happened so fast and he wanted to know the finer details, so they had a meal the next night in the local pub and she described Abersoch and 'her' cottage and the village. Growing up in Liverpool, Joel had been, with his family, to Butlins at Pwllheli , so at least he knew where Abersoch was, although only from a distance.

Ella told him she was so sure about the whole feel of the cottage and the village that she had acted on her gut instinct – it all just felt right.

Once he had the full picture he was delighted for her and offered to help her in her move.

"Apart from anything I want to be your very first guest," he laughed.,

"I shan't be moving much, Joel, but I'd love you to help. Really, once I've got Bones in the car, there is very little room for anything and I feel all I am taking would fit in your Disco, and of course, you shall be my first guest. Who else?"

He walked her back home and, over coffee, discussed what she would take with her. It really boiled down to her personal stuff and pots and pans etc., but, of course, the tapestries were going with her and the bits and pieces she had acquired to match up with them. All the furnishing were either to modern or too large for her new home and they would never have suited her new life anyway.

What Ella really loved was old and treasured furniture and she had a longing to paint and restore things she would find at fairs and junk shops.

She and Joel did a sort of valuation, of the expensive modern things Sam and her bought, and Joel promised to discuss the price with the couple who wanted to buy the apartment.

Chapter 30

Sure enough, true to his word, he rang her a few days later. Could Nathan and his partner come to have a good look again and see if they could buy the furnishings? They came one evening – all three and by the time they left it had all been decided. She let them have the place for a fair price and asked very little for all the other things. They had already done their homework about a mortgage and would have a buyers' survey done and, hopefully, all could complete by the end of the year.

Ella gave in her notice to Mr Asquith, who had half-expected some such move and was most understanding. He and his wife asked all about her future plans and said they would give her an excellent reference, and two weeks later, she was unemployed.

It was a very strange feeling and she was rather lost. All she could do was wait for solicitors and banks and she couldn't settle to anything.

She realized that her mother knew nothing of this huge decision she had taken, so she rang to tell her all about it. To her delight her mother was really encouraging and interested. She was stunned that Sam had left Ella in such a wonderful financial position and Ella felt a small glimmer of amusement at how this had obviously elevated his status in her mother's eyes. She also had a little chat to Charles, as warm and friendly as ever and told him her plans to move in the New Year.

"That sounds terrific, Ella," he said. There was a short pause, while he must have consulted her mother and then he asked, "So what are you doing for Christmas?"

Christmas had never even entered her thoughts and now, when it did, her heart plunged. What would it be like without Sam? She didn't dare imagine.

There was a silence before Charles spoke again.

"Well, why don't you come to visit us? It is a lovely and traditional feast here and it would be such a pleasure to see you again, please say you will?"

She was shaken to the core. "Give me a while and I'll call," she said, to give herself time to think.

She made a coffee and sat at the window. The more she thought of Christmas on her own the more she just dreaded the idea. She knew Joel was on duty all over the holiday and the first week of January, when she hoped to move. It did sound tempting, if only to get away from too many memories of last year.

She'd never flown on her own, but then again she'd never bought a house on her own, either. There was a lot of room for thought. She decided to sleep on it.

And sleep on it she did and made up her mind. She would spend Christmas with her mother and Charles and be home to see in the New Year with Joel. She rang her mother, who sounded genuinely delighted.

"If you get a flight to Bordeaux we can pick you up." she said, "We are about an hour away. It should be mild, but on the other hand it sometimes is quite cold mid-winter, so come prepared. Don't leave it to the last minute, if you're not going to be working. Come a few days before and we can prepare for Christmas together.

The next day, Ella went online and booked herself on a flight from Bristol to Nantes, on 21st December and felt a little stirring of excitement.

When she told Will he asked if she would be away long.

"Only about a week. I want to be home for New Year's Eve to meet up with Joel.

"That's great, because I had wondered if you two would like to have a meal here with me on New Year's Eve, if you have other plans we can rearrange. Have a word with Joel."

The next time she saw her pal she mentioned it.

"Do you know, that sounds great," he said immediately. "All the pubs and restaurants will be heaving and I really enjoy Will's company, and yours too," he hastily grinned. "If Will is cooking tell him I'll take care of the booze then I can kip at your place afterwards."

So there it was – sorted.

Mr and Mrs Asquith took her for afternoon tea on The Crescent and gave her a leaving gift of a lookalike Fabergé egg that picked up all the shades she loved.   It was really exquisite and they were delighted she loved it so much.

"Do write or ring sometimes," Mrs Asquith bid her and she promised she would.

The next few weeks flew.   She had very little to do towards her move, but she cleaned the apartment thoroughly and did a bit of Christmas shopping – just Ma and Charles, Joel and Will and something special for Sam's parents.   She arranged a delivery of flowers every month of the next year – abundant flowers such as Mrs Patel would enjoy.   One day whilst she was shopping she spotted a coat in a window.   It was a deep vibrant green ankle-length and roomy and she fell for it.   It seemed a bit out of her price range, but then she took hold of herself.   She could afford it – why not?   Sam had loved her in greens.   It enveloped her and comforted her and she also felt rather elegant in it and it cheered her up.

She packed what she needed as hand luggage and caught a bus to Bristol Airport, just about 12 miles south of the city.   It was only a smallish airport and many of her fellows were off on skiing trips.   It was an uneventful flight and they landed late afternoon, just as dusk was falling.   She was in France and the air that met them was on the chilly side and she was glad of her big coat.

Very shortly, she was walking through Arrivals to be met, very warmly, by Charles and her mother.   Her mother gave her a really big hug.

"Oh, it is so good to see you.   You look fabulous in that colour, but you've lost a lot of weight.   We'll have to fatten you up.   Charles is a brilliant cook and we eat well here.   Come on, let's get you home," and she pulled Ella's arm through hers and lead her out to the car.

It was dark before they arrived, but lights had been left on outside the house, which was near the middle of a small village, with parking for the car at the side.   It seemed a solid stone-built place and the front door opened into a square hall, with a stone-flagged floor and a wonderful smell of cooking permeated the place.

Charles gave her a kiss and said, "Make yourself at home, you really are so very welcome," and she felt it.   Her mother was so much more relaxed and she actually wore jeans and a big sweater. Ella was amazed.   She was a new woman and a happy one at that.

"Come here, let me look at you. Oh, you've been through a dreadful time and we are both so very sorry. Perhaps a holiday here will help to get you back on your feet. Come and see our little domain."

With that, she guided Ella into a low-ceilinged room, with windows at both ends. From there they turned left into a big kitchen, with a table and an Aga. This was where the smell emanated from. For the first time in ages Ella began to actually feel hungry.

Charles said, "I'll take your bag up, Ella – you have a chat with your mum," and he was gone.

"You look well, Ma," she said. "Are you settling in here?"

"Ella, I have never been so happy in my life. Charles is a really good man and looks after me and the locals are very friendly. Charles has quite good French and I am learning. I need to be able to talk to people and shop on my own sometimes. The weather, of course, is milder, and there are very rarely frosts, but it can be very windy in autumn and winter. The summer is pretty warm but not too hot. That's why Charles bought here years ago and he was right."

She paused for breath. "Now tell me about your plans. When do you move and have you anyone to help you? It's a huge thing to do on your own."

So Ella told her about Joel's offer and told her also how she felt she would feel right in Abersoch.

"I need to start over, Ma. I can't go on living on Bath without Sam."

"I can understand. It must all have been a nightmare and I have never had such a good time since I made my mind up to come here."

At which point, Charles reappeared.

"Follow me," he said, and he made his way up a narrow wooden staircase and onto a small landing. "We have just two rooms," he said, "but they both have their own bathroom. I think you will find it a very comfortable bed. The French like their feather mattresses and pillows and I so much agree."

He opened the door onto a room at the front. It was a good size, with painted furniture and a small four-poster and it all looked very welcoming.

"I'm dishing up in 10 minutes," he said, as he closed the door behind him.

Ella pushed open a door, which led into a bathroom with a big, deep and ancient bath. It was a smart room, with red gingham blinds and red towels.

She unpacked her few things, had a quick wash and was downstairs in the kitchen in a few minutes.

"A good old traditional French meal for you, Ella. Coq-au-vin and cheeses. How does that sound?"

It sounded and smelt delicious and Charles filled their glasses with a deep red wine and he lifted his in a toast.

"To Ella and her new life. May she be as happy as we are."

"Thank you. I hope I can eventually."

With that, they all set to.

They sat and chatted, and by the time two bottles had disappeared, what with the wine and the warmth and a good meal, Ella was feeling quite sleepy.

"Time for bed," her mother said.

"Off you go – we'll just clear up and follow you. The local cockerel may wake you, but at least he isn't too early in mid-winter.

Snug in her deep feather bed, Ella just had time to marvel at the difference in her mother before she fell into a deep and untroubled sleep.

Sure enough, she was wakened by a strange sound. It was the cockerel, but it was about 8 am, just the right time for an alarm.

She lay for a few moments before hearing a door close downstairs. She looked out of her high level window and saw Charles stride down the lane, carrying a basket. She was looking out at a row of cottages that seemed similar to the one she was in. They were all painted in a variety of pastel colours and all had shutters. Behind them seemed to be trees and green space. It was sunny, an early watery sun. She suddenly wanted to see where she was and had a quick shower and dragged on a pair of jeans and made her way downstairs with her long hair bundled up in a red towel. Now she realized there was a very pretty courtyard to the rear and lots of tubs. There were walls all round and lots of plants growing up them. Just a few were in flower, but it was all very attractive.

Her mother was in the kitchen, with a big pot of coffee on the hob.   They sat with a mug each until Charles came back.   He had been for bread and new-laid eggs which they ate with relish.   The butter was salty and Ella could have eaten it all day.

Then they all put jerseys on and went out to have an explore of this little place.   They were in a lane just off the high street and there was a church, two cafes, a butcher and a baker and a general store. The fish man called once a week and the locals brought surplus fruit and veg to be sold at the general store, so they were fine for all day-to-day stuff.   If they needed the town of Pompadour was not very far.

"We'll take you there tomorrow, for the last market before Christmas," she was told.

The day passed very pleasantly and the next morning they drove to Pompadour– a great bustle of markets and traffic and people.   Ella loved it.   They browsed the streets, buying bits and pieces and she marvelled at the terrific displays of fruit and vegetables.   Some stalls sold just one kind of vegetable – a table full of garlic, or baskets of different apples.   Although you couldn't say it was warm, it was sunny and mild and they sat with coffee watching men in berets and scarves at their age-old game of boules.

She discovered that the big meal was on Christmas Eve locally and they were joining up with another couple at a local restaurant before going to Midnight Mass.   It was all within walking distance and it was really quite magical as they wandered through the village, replete after a good meal of roast pheasant.   It seemed that almost all the village was on its way to church and the bells were pealing.   The fact that there was a bright moon added to it all and Ella felt really relaxed and glad she had made the effort.   Outside, there was a lot of happy chat and she was able to manage a little of her basic French and people were delighted.

Christmas Day was quite English.   They had goose and exchanged gifts and drank good wine and brandy and listened to carols on CDs.   Her mother was a new woman and obviously happy and wanted to know all about her cottage and the place she had chosen to live.   Charles had been nearby once, on a golfing trip, and he knew how glorious the area was.

"Once you're settled, what are you going to do?"

"Well, I have a bit of a dream of maybe some part-time job –

there are lots of artistic things going on," she said, "and I would like to try to use my sewing skills in some way as well."

"Sounds good to me – anyway, the best of luck with the idea." He was always interested and encouraging.

"Perhaps, when you are settled, we could come to see you? Are there any hotels close by?"

"Oh, yes. There's one just down the road where I stayed myself."

"That's settled then – whenever you feel ready to show us your place – just let us know. We might catch a ferry and drive up and see some old friends while we're around."

All this made her realize that it wasn't just a pipe dream. She actually was the owner of a Welsh cottage in a delightful place. Her heart lifted.

I'm forging on, Sam, I won't let you down, she thought.

She could think of Sam now without dissolving into tears. She tried to draw strength from the memory of him and of the wonderful life they had, all too briefly, shared. She knew what it was like to be loved truly and she reckoned that some people never knew that love.

Chapter 31

Once back in Bath, refreshed and full of energy, she did her final sorting out and had some cards printed with a photo of Abersoch and her new address and gave them to the few people she had in her life. She also posted a few, with a brief explanation, to Myra, Joanne, Mike and Netta. She had not kept in touch with anyone else from her uni days.

Before New Year arrived she had a long conversation with Sam's parents, who were kind and supportive. Then, on New Year's Eve she, Joel and Will had an excellent meal and quite a lot to drink and a great farewell evening. They went out to watch the fireworks and exchange greetings with some of the neighbours before she and Joel weaved their way upstairs.

She slept heavily and awoke with a start. Then she remembered. This was the day of the start of her new life. Once Joel had had a bacon buttie and coffee he was ready for the road. Her belongings fitted into his 4x4 and she had Bones for company and off they set.

They arranged to meet at the pub in Welshpool for some lunch and arrived within ten minutes of each other. The roads were very quiet and it was a fine, cold day. She introduced Joel to Jenny, who served them a hearty meal and she gave Jenny a card and off they set again.

She was so glad it was a good day, as it really mattered to her that Joel's first impression of Abersoch was a good one. They met up again in Pwllheli so that he could follow her and she pulled over as soon as they cleared Llanbedrog and could see out over the bay. She ran back to his car while Bones had a stroll around.

"Well?" she questioned.

"My God – what a view," Joel said as he climbed out. The sun was low by now and the mountains across the bay stood out clearly in the cold air. The sea was calm – a grey blue of winter. She showed him the islands (as if she owned them) and they stood to drink it all in.

Right – now for my cottage, she thought. *Yes, my cottage.*
He was bowled over when they arrived. Her pal Tudor had let himself in, with her spare key, and there was a fire lit and a fresh loaf on the table. Already it felt like home.

Bless you, Tudor, she thought. He had left a little note of welcome and an invitation to a meal, if they weren't too tired. The adrenalin was flowing and they did a quick unpack and a good inspection of the place. They draped the bedding around to unchill and then wrapped up and put Bones on his lead and went to have a look at the place where she was going to live.

The shops were all closed, as it was New Year's Day, but there were people about – all locals – and all spoke to them. Joel was fascinated by the lifeboat house, and the glorious beach – in fact he was delighted by it all and Ella's little doubts floated away in a euphoric cloud. She had done right. Now she was certain.

Tudor welcomed her as a long-term friend and he and Joel hit it off instantly. He gave them a Thai feast and then they walked back up the hill – ready for their beds. She had had a few basics delivered – two single beds and a hefty pine table. They made up the two beds and she opened a window a little bit to see if she could hear the sea, but it was still and quiet.

When she woke, Joel was busy relighting the fire and they sat by it with coffee and toasted the bread she had brought. While they sat she explained her plans for the cottage. She would just camp in it as she gradually turned into exactly what she wanted. She needed to get the feel and oversee the work and Joel quite agreed.

This room would stay as it was, but the opposite room she wanted to make into two, by adding a wall and a window. She could then have a little workroom. If possible she wanted to build out at the rear of the kitchen, making it large enough for a large table and perhaps a settee. She could see it all in her mind's eye.

They had a walk around her little piece of land. They were both clueless about gardens, but thought a few smallish trees at the far end might be fruit trees. It would be a case of seeing what happened in the spring.

Joel left late morning – back on duty on 3rd January and with a fair drive ahead. He kissed her and gave her a long hug.

"I'm just at the end of a phone," he said, "and I shall be back soon. In fact, I may treat this as my seaside holiday home."

They both laughed.

"Whenever," Ella said. "You know you are my best friend in the whole world and I need you, Joel."

She fought back tears and he did the same.

"Hopefully the work will be cracking on when you see it again."

Another hug by the gate and he was gone.

Ella walked slowly back up the path. What now? She decided to keep busy, so she jumped in the car and went to do some shopping. She found a large Spar shop and bought lots of basic necessities, plus a box of Malteasers and then sat by the fire and began to draw up plans.

She didn't feel scared on her own somehow. The place seemed to sit safely around her and she went to bed planning some walls in the morning.

Shortly after she was up, her phone rang. It was Gaynor Ackersley from the agents'. The office was shut until the weekend, but she wanted to know if everything was OK and if Ella was finding her way around.

Ella told her she had done a bit of shopping and was making plans for the cottage.

"Do you have any local tradesmen you could recommend?" she enquired.

"Oh yes," said Gaynor. "Dai Evans is your man – a jack of all trades, but good at them all. Honest as the day and he won't take you for a ride. Shall I get him to give you a call?"

"Oh, yes, please. The sooner the better," and they left it like that.

Two hours later, her mobile went again.

"Is that Miss Hodson?" enquired a man with a very strong Welsh accent. "This is Dai Evans. Gaynor told me you have some work you need doing and I am having a break for a week or so, so I thought I'd give you a call.

"I'm glad you did, Mr Evans. Could you come up and have a look whenever it suits you?"

"What about tomorrow at 10 o'clock? I know where you are," he laughed.

During the night the wind blew up and, as she waited by the window, in the morning, a yellow van pulled up and a stocky figure climbed out, pulling a woolly hat over his ears and battled up the path.

She opened the door before he got there and held out her hand.

"Come in, do, Mr Evans. It's wild out there," and he stepped in.

As he pulled off his hat and ran his fingers across his hair she realized he was probably in his fifties.

"I'm Dai, Miss Hodson," he grinned. "No-one calls me Mr Evans, not even the bobby."

"Well, I would rather be called by my name, too – it's Ella."

"Well, there's a good name for you. I'm a big fan of Ella Fitzgerald, are you?" and that was it – they were off. It turned out he was in a local jazz group where he played the trombone and she told him her Dad had rebelled against her other Christian names.

Heavens, thought Ella, *I feel as if I known this man for years.*

He followed her round all the rooms and then went round again, making copious notes, on the back of an old envelope. Then they sat with a mug of tea.

"I like builders tea," Dai said, "if you don't mind. Strong and sweet and milky."

He knew the old man who had lived here, but had never been in. He saw the potential right away and said his son, young Dai, was very good at doing simple drawings, good enough to save her using an architect.

"I would suggest you keep any extension of the kitchen within the area allowed without having to have planning permission and then it is all plain sailing. As the house has never had work done to extend the place you'll get away with it fine."

So the decision was made. Was she daft? Should she be getting more estimates? Ella decided to go on her gut instinct. She asked Dai to get his son to do some drawings and then give her an estimate. It was going to be a big job for Dai and son, but it was the quietest time of their year and they could do it as soon as she was agreed.

Young Dai, it transpired, was doing an apprenticeship in carpentry and did one day a week at college in Caernarvon. When his dad wasn't too busy he did some work for the craft outlet further down the road.

"Quite a lot of us turn our hands to a few things around here," Dai told her. "We're all pretty self-sufficient. You have to be when the place can be crazy in summer and very quiet in winter. What do you do, Miss?"

She told him that she was into art and embroidery and had worked in a museum, but that she had chosen to have a complete break and start again. *He would probably deduce a broken love affair*, she thought.

"Well now – I suppose you know of Plas Glen-y-Wyddw?" he asked. "That'll be right up your street. We're very proud of it round here, although I'm not very arty myself.

Puzzled, Ella asked, "You mean that pub on the bend at Llanbedrog?"

Dai roared laughing, "No, I don't see you as a barmaid somehow, I meant the big house in the vale behind the pub. That's the same name – both named from the same person. The big house is an art gallery, quite famous, it is, but I don't think it will be open now. In fact, quite a few businesses shut down early in the year for their holidays, as it can get pretty busy later in the season."

When he'd gone, Ella wandered around the cottage. She had a fire lit to warm the place, but it suddenly felt very empty. She decided she must get out – weather or not. Bones had on a waterproof jacket, as he got cold easily and, once they were both wrapped up, off they went. It was really wet and on the way she had a look at the row of little craft outlets – all closed for January and she couldn't see much through shuttered windows. There wasn't even a view – the rain was too heavy and she realized, once in the village, that the tide was in, as all she could see was water – quite rough-looking grey water. There was a ringing sound from the masts of the boats bobbing about by the bridge where the river met the sea and a deserted air about the place. She found a few shops open and bought a paper and looked for somewhere to have coffee, without much luck.

Am I crazy, she wondered. *It's all so very different from Bath, which is always open and busy.* Bones didn't like the weather and was soaked, so they retraced their steps back up the hill. She felt very alone and had to fight hard not to give in to weeping.

Chapter 32

The following day was no different. They went up the lane this time, but all they saw were sheep huddled against the stone walls and trees growing over away from the wind.

What have I done? she thought. *Have I made a huge mistake?* Then, on the way back she saw a figure near her gate. In a long raincoat and a sou'wester she couldn't tell if it was a man or a woman. She wondered where they could be going and realized they would meet near her gate. The figure slowed as they approached and she saw it was a woman, with a basket over her arm.

"Good day to you, are you the lady who has bought Evan's cottage? I am just on my way to see you. Bethan Jones – how are you?" she babbled in her lovely Welsh voice. "What a day we've chosen – we must both be mad," and she laughed. "I'm your nearest neighbour, so I thought I would come and say hello and welcome."

"Oh, thank you – won't you come in – the fire's lit," said Ella, a bit nonplussed. There was no furniture or curtains or anything really. She hadn't reckoned on visitors, but what could she do? She opened the gate and walked ahead up the path and turned the key. A welcome blast of warm air greeted them and they were in.

"I'm afraid I only have a couple of chairs as yet," she began.

"Oh, don't you be worrying – we all start somewhere. I've brought you some home made soup and one of my Bara Briths," as she lifted them onto the table. "It's a day for soup."

She was a tall, strong-looking woman, with greying hair in a plait.

"Please – do take your wet coat off," Ella said and they both hung the dripping coats on hooks on the door. She removed the dog's coat and he spread out in front of the fire.

"Would you like coffee or tea?"

"Coffee would be lovely, my dear," and off she went to make it, followed by her new friend, who was obviously a relaxed, chatty woman. When they had settled by the fire, she said, "So, and your name is Ella and the dog is Bones. Just you two is it? It's a good home you've chosen. I raised three children here – all gone now – it's a good place to live is this."

As she babbled Ella began to realize you couldn't help but warm to this chatty woman with a warm heart and she was feeling a little less anxious.

"You've chosen a poor time of year to move. The place must feel dead to a young girl like you at this time of year, and the place will feel empty and chilly until you've got your curtains up and things sorted."

Hearing her doubts put into words made the worry recede a bit. "Yes, I think you've hit the nail on the head. Do you mind if I call you Bethan?"

"Mind? I'd feel strange if you didn't. I'm the newly retired midwife around here and everyone calls me Bethan. I'm Bethan the babies in the village," and they both laughed. "So, what brought you here, you're obviously not Welsh?" She was so artless you couldn't feel she was being nosy.

"Oh, I just wanted a big change of scene and I fancied the sea," which seemed enough for now. "What did you call your cake?" she changed the subject.

"Bara Brith, dear. It's a sort of tea bread, but spicy – great well buttered. I'll give you a recipe when you're more settled.

They chatted on for a while before she shrugged back into her Barbour. "Dewi will be wanting his lunch," and off she went.

Ella felt much more cheerful when she had gone and then the rain eased. *Curtains,* she thought, *I need curtains,* and she got out her tape measure and began to make notes.

The days and weeks went by. She explored the shops and the market for fabrics and made curtains for the living room and one bedroom and a blind for the bathroom. It was her first attempt at a blind and she was really pleased with it. The curtains in the living room took some doing, as she lined them with a really heavy cloth. She kept to the colours in her cushions and tapestry – all still stored away in black bin liners. Because of the work she wanted done she left the other windows.

One day she had a call from the planning officer on the local council and he seemed quite satisfied with her plans and, towards the end of her first month, Dai and young Dai moved in. It was

131

company and she shared a brew sometimes with them, and Dai regaled her with village gossip and tales. His boy was quite shy, but had a lovely smile and she was kept busy by them asking her opinions and making drinks.

She was starting to recognise folk. She bumped into Gaynor now and then and saw Bethan often and had met her Dewi while walking the dog. Dewi was quite taciturn compared to his voluble wife and just passed the time of day.

She shopped at the smaller shop right in the village and used the butcher for the infrequent meat meals she had, because she took advantage of a local fish delivery Bethan told her about, she walked a lot and people began to get used to her and Bones would speak to her n passing. Gradually her fears grew less and she began to think that perhaps she had made a good decision after all.

The lifeboat station intrigued her and, when she saw a poster for a Beer and Bingo to support the RNLI, she plucked courage and asked Bethan if she would be going.

"Going," said Bethan. "In the winter, we go to every social event there is," and off they went, with Dewi in quiet attendance, to the village hall. Sure enough, the place was packed. They kept it simple. There were canned beers and sausage barm cakes and a raffle. The atmosphere was noisy and friendly and she saw a few faces she recognised. Tudor was working, but had donated a voucher for the raffle. After a couple of cans Dewi relaxed a bit and told her he was nearing retirement, but drove buses on the peninsula.

"Been here man and boy – all my life," he told her. He had been dragged away on holiday by Bethan a few times but didn't rate anywhere better than his home village. That was quite reassuring to Ella and she began to enjoy herself. She had to listen hard, as the man calling had a very strong accent and a lot of the chat was in Welsh, but as Bethan said there were quite a few 'incomers' in the village and they all switched languages accordingly. However, they were very proud of being in an area that was one of the strongholds of the ancient language.

"It's a language of poets and singers," Bethan told her, "and we are the people who have to keep it alive."

To general hilarity, Ella won a rustic, hand painted sign. In Welsh, it said, 'Cymru'. It seemed most appropriate and she had Dai

132

junior make a little scaffold to hang it near the gate. Welcome.

She began to worry about Bones. He ate even less and seemed to be lethargic. She asked around and discovered there was a vet the other side of town (as the locals referred to Pwllheli). At certain times you could just walk in. So, one morning, she persuaded the dog into her car and went off to find the vet. It was a purpose-built and smart building and she was told she was number 3 in line. An old man with an older dog went in and a lady with a little bird in a cage. Then it was their turn. Somehow she expected the vet to be middle-aged or older, but it was a young man who held his hand out. So this was Mr Parry-Jones, as she had read on the door.

"What can we do for you, old man?" he asked as he bent over to rub Bones' ear. He had a very deep, gentle voice and the skinny old dog relaxed a bit.

Ella told him why she was concerned and he asked her a few questions. He had thick, wavy, black hair and dark blue eyes and was very tall and broad.

He lifted Bones on to his table and had a good look at him.

"What age is he?" he said.

Ella confessed she was only guessing.

"We were told he was about seven and we've had him about two years," the 'we' just slipped out. "Is he ill?"

"I feel he is just getting weary – his heartbeat is weak and his pulse is slow. If, as you say, he has raced, that tells on them in later years, I'm afraid. After all, he could be ten or so and that's a good age for his breed. I can liven him up a bit with a few pills, but it won't keep him going forever, I'm afraid. Anyway, see how he goes and have a chat to your partner about what you will want for him."

He smiled kindly and patted her arm as she stood and, as she paid, she realized that he thought she had someone in her life that she could talk to. It upset her, as did the verdict on Bones and it was a sad drive home.

Chapter 33

Meanwhile, the newly-altered cottage was taking place around her. Dai and Dai were good, steady workers and she enjoyed their company.

One day, after weeks of work, when young Dai was at college his dad suddenly said, over their mugs of tea, "So what's your story, Ella? What's a lovely young girl doing here on her own with an old whippet?"

And she told him. There was a long silence, then Dai pushed his chair back and stood with his hand on her shoulder. "I'm so very, very sorry, lass. You've been to Hell and back. I hope this place heals your soul."

She thought, *It's right, the Welsh do have a way with words.*

For a couple of days, he was quieter, as if he was worried about disturbing her privacy, but before too long, he was whistling and singing as he worked and she was so glad.

The big extension at the back of the house was nearly done and it was time to look for kitchen fittings.

She decided that what few cupboards and shelves she wanted could be made by young Dai and he made a superb job of it, using reclaimed timbers, so that if felt as if it had been there for ever. There was a large window looking out towards the sea and a wood-burning stove to heat the water. For winter she had some radiators fitted, but she hoped to keep it simple. The bathroom was refitted and work was going on on the interior wall. Soon it would be time to furnish it and she felt a fission of excitement at all that would entail. She had begun to look around and had found a good, large antique shop in Porthmadog, about 40 minutes' drive away. There were also a few, smaller outlets with all sorts of interesting items and, gradually, she began to make her house into a home. She knew that when she had finished the job she had some very serious decisions to make and tried not to think too far ahead.

She loved the weeks she had with her dog and began to pull

strands of wool out of hedges and fences, with a long-term view of learning to spin. She had already been taught the rudiments of carding etc., and she accumulated a bag of wool and stored it in the outhouse, which she had found was dry.

March lived up to its name and was a wild month. The sea pounded in onto the shore and she could hear it and, sometimes, even feel it. It was exhilarating and different. She skipped beach walks for a while, as Bones trembled at the ferocity of the waves.

One day, she noticed shoots coming through the grass and by the end of the month, there were daffodils opening all over the garden. Ella was thrilled. *I must learn what to do with this land*, she thought. There was a fair-sized plot really, as it went right round the house. She had decided against having a garage build, mostly because there was at least one window in every wall and the outhouse was large enough for any bits and pieces.

With the daffodils came the visitors – slowly at first and building up. Mike came to stay for a night and fell in love with the place. He had a greenkeeper's job at St David's, further south and was still fancy free. He told her that his sister, Cara, had told the family she was buying an apartment to share with her female partner, with whom she hoped to spend her life. After the initial shock the had all adjusted and supported her.

"Yes, your family would do," Ella said. "My mother would have died at the shame of it," they both laughed.

They had a drink and a pub meal and Ella heard someone talk about the lifeboat station. At the end of the month it would be open on a Thursday evening and she resolved to be there. As they strolled back, a tall figure went by. As he saw her, he said, "Hi, how's the old dog? Still OK?" and she realized it was the vet.

"Yes, thanks, he's alright, but slowing down," and they went on their way.

The next time she bumped into him was at the open evening at the lifeboat station. She was poking around, taking it all in when he came out of a door marked 'Crew Only'.

Ah, she thought. *He must be involved.*

While she had tea and biscuits and bought some postcards she had a chat to two of the ladies who were serving. She asked them if they needed any more voluntary help and they said that they had enough at the moment, but one never knew.

"Whereabouts are you living?" one asked and when she told her she said, "Well, give me your phone number – you're certainly close by. Would you be available to fill in at short notice?" and Ella said she would. It was a first little step to getting more involved in the life of the place.

Easter came and so did the people. Suddenly, Abersoch was buzzing and busy. Every shop was open, as well as all the cafes and bars and there were people everywhere.

Bethan and Dewi invited her to tea on Easter Sunday. It was a family tradition and Ella felt very honoured. She met the two daughters and one son. The girls were married and one of them had a toddler and a new baby. She was about Ella's age.

"We aim to have another one in about 2 years and I shall be a stay-at-home mum until they all start school. Time enough then for me to go back to my nursing job," she told Ella.

Bethan must have been baking for days and there was a terrific spread. They ate themselves to a standstill and then they had a sing-song. Dewi played the piano quite well and to Ella their combined voices were wonderful.

When she commented, the boy said, "If you're Welsh, you need to sing. It's just in your genes." He was away at uni in the north, but was aiming to come home at the end of his course.

"I'm doing Graphic Design," he said. "If I can't find work here, I may have to go as far as Chester." He said this as if Chester was a thousand miles away.

"I feel I will settle here," Ella told him. "I hated Corby, where I was raised. Then I lived in Bristol and Bath, which were really great, but this is beginning to feel like home."

"You've moved about a bit then."

"Well, uni and then a job. I've only been abroad once," she said.

"I had a gap year and managed to get a poorly paid job in San Francisco for most of it – what a place that is. I hope it looks good on my CV! It was a bit of an eye-opener after Abersoch. I had a room in a hostel and there were some pretty dubious people about," he laughed. "It taught me how to streetwise, anyway. The villains of Abersoch can do their worst," and they both laughed.

"Seriously, is there much crime here? I really don't imagine it."

"Well, there are always a few dodgy people anywhere. Mostly, it's to do with boats and not big stuff. The police aren't run off their feet, anyway."

"Hope to see you again, then she reluctantly tore herself away.

"I may never eat again," she told Bones as they settled by the fire.

Chapter 34

Sometimes the days dragged and she knew she had to find something to fill the hours. First of all, she went to the craft shops and asked the photographer if he had any jobs going.

"Sorry, I don't really have much staff, nothing at present, but give me your number anyway." His photographs filled the walls and were absolutely amazing.

"Of course you can browse all you want. There are more upstairs."

She had never seen such dramatic photos.

"Thank you, I'll come back soon," she said. She didn't want to make any quick decisions. She walked back and studied her walls for quite a while.

Joel rang frequently and came to stay for a few days. He had only been in early January and saw a different place. The boats were back on their moorings near the yacht club and there were a couple of brave wind surfers. Once on the beach he was like a child and had to test the water. He rolled his jeans up and was in shin deep – but not for long.

"God, it's cold," he said. "No wonder there are so many shops selling wet suits – and what's this Wakestock Festival I am seeing posters for?"

They asked Tudor.

"Don't even think about it," he said. "It's madness for the very young – sorry, Joel, but you're way too old. The village will be like a nut house that weekend. Most of them camp out and it's sure to rain and they pile in to find a hot meal! Good for business but mad!"

"Now, if you want to see Abersoch enjoying itself, you need to come for the jazz weekend." Joel's ears pricked up.

"You have a jazz festival?"

"Oh, yes, and a very good one, too – plenty of big names and all very civilized. At least the drunks are adults!"

Ella didn't know any of this.   *I have a lot to learn,* she considered.

Tudor gave them the details and Joel decided he would return – if he was welcome.

"If Ella doesn't want you, you can always bunk here," Tudor laughed, and so that was settled.

Joel and Ella had a day out to explore a place near to Porthmadog, called Portmerion, and had a fascinating explore of this magical place and its hidden coves.   They had a meal that evening in the hotel, watching the tides reclaim the miles of golden sands.

She talked to Joel about Bones. He could see his life was ebbing. She had never realized how fond she had grown of this funny-looking dog.

She also discussed with him the really big decision she was going to have to make. It helped to be able to talk.

By summer, she knew Bones had had enough. As it got warmer, he was more breathless and he scarcely ate.   She gathered all her strength and rang the vets. The receptionist was very kind and very helpful.   Ella could take him there, or the vet would come out. What should she do? She thought about it and realized she couldn't cope with another death in her home. She rang back and within two days it was all over and Ella had a little box, all that remained of Bones.   She missed him so much and she cried many bitter tears. She couldn't be bothered to eat properly and was sinking pretty low when she had a call. One of the ladies on the lifeboat volunteers had taken ill and could she help keep this Thursday? It shook her out of her misery and she pulled herself together and made tea and washed up.   To her total delight the boat was launched, as a windsurfer was in trouble and she felt involved.   The other lady filled her in a bit about the crew, all of whom were volunteers.   The retiring age was only 45, so it was a job for a young man. They had to live and work within a short distance. They were no longer summoned by the 'boom', it was hi-tech now and they had personal bleepers. A few, who worked outside of the 5 minute call out signed on for the days and evenings when they were readily available and they always managed to turn out a full crew within minutes.   It was an inshore boat – a huge R1B, because they were not in a shipping lane, but in an enormous bay.   It was all very interesting to Ella and it helped take her mind off her loss.

True to his word, Joel appeared for the jazz in June. The two of them had a ball. Once he heard about the procession he insisted they do up umbrellas and join in. Ella knew that when medics let their hair down they really do and Joel became a bit of a legend that weekend. Late at night they went down to the beach and threw the contents of the little box into the light breeze and she cried on Joel's shoulder. Another part of her had gone missing.

Chapter 35

The house was more or less done – Bones had gone. Was it, she wondered, time for the next step? Time – she needed lots of time to consider everything.

While she was thinking she bought a very large print, on canvas, of sunset on the Llyn. She hung it in her living room and really appreciated it. Every month she checked her account online. She scarcely made an impression on the cash she had, even after the work on the house. She was solvent, and she was healthy. She mustn't wait too long. She got her box of papers and began to really study them. Joel had warned her it would not be easy.

In the end, he proved correct. He managed to go with her to Manchester, partly to plead her case. She had to have physical examinations, financial examinations, psychological examinations and questions, questions, questions.

Why did she want a child? Why not wait until she met someone – she was still young – had she considered all the implications? Again and again she had to explain herself. Her health was perfect – her financial situation very good, but in the end, it boiled down to this major issue. Why have the child of a dead man?

She had never known she could argue so vehemently. She quite surprised herself. She battled away every obstacle put before her. This brilliant man had wanted a child so much that it had been his dying wish. He had done it all, hoping he would live to see his child, but was cheated of that by death. She was determined she would have their baby – it was her right.

It took a very long time. It was months before she opened a letter one day. Her campaign had been a success and she could make an appointment at St Mary's to begin IVF.

At this point, she confided in Bethan, who was like an aunt by now. Bethan immediately found out all she could about the whole process while she came to terms with this rather startling news. Up to then Ella had told her just a little about her background. When she had done her homework, she said, "Right then, I shall come with you. You need to book into a hotel near St Mary's, as you need to be close by when they do the treatment. You may find some resentment with some people at the hospital. People have their own views on IVF, but I shall be in your corner, Ella – you need someone, and I am pretty clued up about the medical side of it all."

Ella accepted her offer with huge relief. She knew she needed help.

Meanwhile she found some voluntary work at the Art Gallery at Llanbedrog and was then asked if she wanted to work for a salary just over weekends, which were their busiest times. She jumped at the offer. She worked 9-5 at the weekends and earned a very small wage, but she was back in contact with art and hugely enjoyed it. They soon discovered how knowledgeable she was and was given quite a lot of responsibility. As the season for holidaymakers quietened down there were more displays by visiting artists and these went on into winter. There was a pleasant cafe in the conservatory, so she spent most of her weekend there. Between that and the odd fill-in at the lifeboat her life was busier. Strangely, without Bones she walked more – not every day as she had done, but longer walks on the cliffs and never tired of the places she discovered.

In her little car she found places such as Aberdaron and resolved to go to Bardsey one day. The more she saw the more she was sure she had done right. By and large everyone was very welcoming to her. She had one unpleasant experience at the Gallery, but people were friendly and she was getting to be known as a resident, rather than a tourist.

While she awaited a call from St Mary's, she had a call from her mother. Charles had been unwell and had had a pacemaker fitted and seemed fine again. She was well, but slowing down a bit. Would they be welcome to visit in the New Year? Ella hesitated, because she was hoping to go to Manchester in the New Year, but she wasn't ready to confide that piece of news.

"What are you doing for Christmas, Ma? Why don't you come then?"

"Could you cope?" her mother asked. "What about the hotels at that time of year – I'll have to talk to Charles."

Ella promised to check on the hotels and rung her later and she walked down to have coffee with Tudor. He was always open over Christmas, on a B&B basis and had a few rooms available. So Ella rang France.

Charles was keen and they asked her to book them in for 4 nights over Christmas. They would be in touch again soon.

The visit concentrated her mind and she set about finishing various projects around the house. On a visit to the market she bought some handmade decorations and made some of her own.

Bethan promised to make her a pudding while she made her family ones and she began to make lists. After all, she had never really catered for families and never over Christmas.

They decorated the gallery and there was actually a wedding booked in for early December, only the second one since they obtained a license and there were the preparations for that. It was not a large do and the cafe was going to lay on a buffet. The time was now actually going quite fast.

She decided to visit Joel, as he came to her so often. She had very mixed feelings about going back to Bath, but she steeled herself. On the way down, she popped in on The Woolpack for coffee. To her amazement Jenny told her that she and two pals had been at the Wakestock Festival. She'd lost Ella's mobile number and couldn't contact her. They had had a wild time and she had loved the area. She told Ella she was ready for a change. If ever Ella heard of anything suitable in Abersoch, would she let her know?

She drove straight to Joel's flat, which had been tidied up a bit in her honour, and they had a curry and drank lager and caught up. He offered her any support she needed and was relieved to hear that Bethan had her under her wing. The next day, he took her to see Wells Cathedral and they ate out. He carefully avoided places she had been with Sam, for which she was very grateful. She couldn't manage a visit to Will, in their old house, but she rang him the next day and they all had coffee together. He seemed really delighted at all news of her new home and her little job and was enjoying his car.

"Why not give it a real adventure and come to visit me, Will, there's an excellent, reasonable hotel, but leave it until spring. The trip through Snowdonia could be hairy in winter."

After they had coffee she set off again. *I'm going home*, she thought.

Chapter 36

Quite suddenly, her mother's visit was very close. They had decided to bring the car over and would land at Holyhead. Then, later, they were going to see old pals of Charles, so they were making a holiday of it. She made her preparations and nervously awaited the call to say they had arrived on Welsh soil. Charles had sat nav and was confident of finding her cottage. She was so anxious that they would like her new home and life. The cottage looked great. There was a small tree in the living room and lots of candles and her crib in pride of place. She'd cut lots of ivy and it was trailed along the beams and the fire glowed a welcome. There was a lasagne ready to pop in the oven and salads and garlic bread and good red wine open and ready.

She felt a burst of emotion that surprised her, as she ran down the path. It was a fine, crisp day, without the wind that sometimes hurled itself down the lane and, as they got out of the car they stood to take it all in.

"Well," said Charles, "you've certainly found a spectacular part of the world. The drive was quite breathtaking"

Her mother hugged her.

"It seems such a while, Ella. How have you been? You look very well, much better than last time."

They walked slowly up the path, chatting as they went and Ella began to relax. After all this was were mother and she had softened a great deal.

Tea was made and homemade scones appeared, but first they had a good look around. The old place was at its best and they really enthused. They asked lots of questions and admired what work Ella had had done.

"You certainly have an eye for colour and old things," her mother said, "it must be your artistic training. It's so vibrant, but peaceful too."

Charles was more practical and queried her heating system and what she had planned for the garden.

She told them about her little jobs and she would take them to the Gallery tomorrow and they sat talking very comfortably until it was time for them to go to Tudor's place. She drove ahead of them and introduced them all and told them to expect a terrific breakfast. Then she arranged to call for them mid-morning and drove back up the hill, happy with her day. She realized how rarely she had company in the house and resolved to do something about it, in the New Year.

They spent Christmas Eve at the Gallery, with which they were most impressed and joined in the carols sung on the harbour in the evening and visited the little Catholic church for Mass later on.

Tudor joined them for dinner on Christmas Day and they all joined in – knowing it was Ella's first attempt. They had a very amiable meal and beautiful wines and sat around the fire until late.

Annie seemed to hit it off with Tudor and even guessed that he was not (as she said) the marrying kind. On his part he flirted a little with her and talked about France and cars with Charles and eventually it was time for bed. Before they left, Annie said to Ella, "We have had a very happy day, Ella, and you have spoilt us. Thank you dear. But tell me – do you ever get lonely here on your own?"

Ella hesitated. "Yes, sometimes I feel very alone. It would be wonderful to have somebody to talk to, especially in the evening, but most of the time I am content, Ma. I made the right decision for me and who knows what the New Year will bring?"

The visit was a great success and when they had gone, Ella felt at a bit of a loss. The weather had changed and it was very wet and wild and not very suitable for long walks, but one day she was out for a brisk walk on the beach when she realized the lifeboat crew were arriving and dashing out of their cars. She ran back along the shore and was just in time to see the Inshore R1B being towed out to launch. She wondered who would be out today, in this awful weather. There were no small boats visible.

Her curiosity aroused, she clambered up to the station to ask. Apparently it was a call about a climber on the cliff around the headland. She waited and waited as the boat came back, sometimes in view and sometimes hidden in the trough of a huge wave. It hadn't taken long. The teenage had slipped onto rocks at high tide

level and couldn't climb to safety.   He wasn't injured – just very
embarrassed and grateful.   She recognised a couple of the men, but
suddenly she saw the young vet and he smiled across at her as he
jumped off the boat.

Luckily the day after – New Year's Day – was a lot more peaceful
and a couple of hundred hardy souls did a sea dip for local charities.
Tudor was one of them, in fancy dress and it was great fun and very
sociable.

Ella entered a New Year with her head full of different
possibilities. What would this year bring?

She rang Gaynor and they had a girlie night in. Gaynor fetched a
takeaway with her and got a lift from her broker, so they shared a
bottle of wine and a good natter. At least she had made a start.

Chapter 37

Then a very excited and exiting call from Myra came. She and Andrew had had a baby boy, on the day before New Year. He had red hair, like his daddy, and was the most wonderful baby in the whole world. It was such wonderful news and encouraged Ella in her plans.

The letter came in late January and, by mid-February, she and Bethan were installed in an Ibis Hotel in Manchester and she began her treatment. It wasn't very pleasant and she couldn't have coped on her own, but Bethan was an absolute gem. After a couple of quite days, they drove home – and waited.

When Ella began her period, just as usual, she was really distraught and ran down the lane to Bethan's house. It was a huge blow. She had been told not to be too hopeful, but she needed to be hopeful, otherwise she couldn't cope with it all. Bethan got in touch with St Mary's and they gave them another appointment, in April, and off they went again. Ella knew she would only get this IVF treatment once more, after this, and it was a sombre couple of days and a very quiet trip home. Bethan did her best to keep her spirits up, but she was missing Sam far worse than for a long time and was very emotional. Was it all going to fall apart?

She went home and more or less hibernated, as if she had to treat herself as an invalid. Bethan, alone, knew what she was going through and did all she could to help. Joel, of course, was in on the secret, but he was only on the end of a phone line.

By mid-May she dared to hope and by the end of the month she was full of excitement. Back they went – to hear the magic news she was in the very early days of carrying Sam's baby. Her and Sam's baby. She was totally overcome by every emotion in the world. She was thrilled but fearful; excited but concerned. Gradually, her head quietened down and she began to realize this was real. She was going to have a baby. She, Ella, was to be a mother. She rang Joel and laughed and cried. Then she rang Myra. She was stunned at first, but then was so genuinely delighted that she gave Ella heart. She was so full of advice too, and told Ella to ring up whenever. She knew all about the ups and downs of pregnancy – she was now a loving expert.

She didn't tell her mother – that could wait a while!

At the hospital, they told her she should go back to them for her 12 week scan. After that, if all was well, she would be transferred to the care of the nearest antenatal clinic. This, she discovered, was at a cottage hospital the other side of town, but only 15 minutes' drive away.

Bethan was almost as thrilled as she was. She said she would go to Manchester with her for her scan.

It was just as well that she did. The Consultant sat her down and all was well and the scan had shown him two healthy babies. She thought she was hearing things and asked him, "Do you mean I am having twins?"

"Indeed I do," he smiled. "Two for the price of one. You should be fine, a young fit girl like you. They'll keep an eye on you and if the babies grow a bit fast you may be induced, but that's all well in the future. Go home and do all you would normally do, within reason. Pregnancy is not an illness and most young mums enjoy it."

As Bethan said later, "It takes a man who never had morning sickness to say that."

They sat in the coffee shop and Ella was in a state of shock. She had known this was possible, but had never really given it much thought. Two babies – delightful, but how would she cope?

They talked all the way home and it began to seem a reality and the more she began to take it in, the more excited she became. She tried to imagine how it would be.

The most wonderful thought was that her babies would always have somebody very close. Ella had not enjoyed being an only one. She would have a family.

Her morning nausea wasn't too bad and didn't last too long and, by the time she was summoned to antenatal she felt really well.

She did wonder whether she would be treated any differently, because of her situation, but the only thing the midwife was concerned about was the health of her and her babies. She was given a date in mid-November and another appointment for two months off.

Her next visit was when she would be shown the maternity wards etc. and could bring her partner if she wished. Oh, how she did wish, but she kept positive, especially when a little flutter, like a butterfly, caused her to catch her breath one afternoon on the beach.

She talked to Myra, who said that she really would need some help, if only in the first few months.

"It can be hard enough, sometimes when it's 2-1, but I really can't imagine 1-2!"

Bethan more or less said the same thing.

Then Ella had a brain wave. How about approaching Jenny, who was looking for a change.

Instead of ringing her, she decided to visit, without Jenny being interrupted by customers.

She heard back within days. Jenny was thrilled she had thought of her and would jump at the chance. Could she come up her next weekend off and they could really discuss it all – and she arrived the next week.

She was so thrilled that Ella had confided in her and felt she was so brave. If she could help her it would be a joy and she so obviously meant it that Ella was very touched.

Jenny confessed to knowing very little about babies and Ella told her she had no experience herself. Ella rang Bethan and she asked them both for tea and cakes. She so obviously wanted to give Jenny the once-over, and she seemed to pass scrutiny because Bethan told them that very few young first time parents know much about babies.

"Read some good parenting books and remember babies are tougher than they look. They need food, warmth, lots of love and a steady, caring hand and you two will manage very well. Remember I am only down the road if you ever do panic. Try to have a reasonably regular routine, but don't try for perfection. You'll all learn together."

Jenny went off home to give her Dad fair warning and said she would move up to Abersoch in September.

When Ella realized her little bump was going to give her secret away, she began to tell the people she cared most about and was met with delight, as well as a few curious questions.

Gaynor was fascinated, but proved to be very supportive and immediately bought baby wool.

Tudor was delighted for her. When he heard about Jenny, he said he might be able to give her a little bar work. He was also interested in how she found herself the expectant mother of twins, as a single girl. If anyone was shocked or disapproving, they didn't say so in front of Ella. Although she knew there would be talk behind her back from some in the village, but she had enough friends now, who were on her side.

Chapter 38

When she got to the end of her second trimester, she decided it was time to ring her mother. She put it off for days, but plucked up courage early one morning, before she talked herself out of it.

There was a long silence and Ella was obliged to ask, "Are you still there, Ma?"

"Well, yes I am, but I'm speechless. I'll ring you back," and the phone went down.

It was an hour before it rang. Her mother asked her all sorts of questions, initially supposing that Ella had a new boyfriend and it all took an awful lot of explaining. Ella was worn out and tearful by the time she put the receiver down.

However, that same evening, there was another call from France, this time from Charles.

"Your mother was knocked for six," he told Ella, "and upset at the thought of all you are going through all alone. How are you going to manage, Ella?"

She explained her plans to this kind man and he seemed to accept that she had gone into all this of her own free will, knowing she could manage and longing to fulfil Sam's dream. As they talked, she could sense his attitude softening and, in the end, he said he would explain it all to Annie and he was pretty sure she would accept it in time.

"You must realize, Ella, that your mother's values were learned a long time ago and she can be pretty unmoving, but I will do my best. All the luck in the world. Keep in close touch," and he was gone.

True to her word, Jenny arrived in early September and moved into the small room downstairs. She said she would have a baby alarm in her room too, as she wanted to do all she could. She put her own stuff around her room and very soon made herself at home and it was great to have company and somebody else to cook for, although she did her fair share. They had trips out to shop for baby things and bought two cradles in Porthmadog. Bethan had advised

151

sharing a larger cot, when the time came and to leave the babies together until they outgrew it, as they would settle better. They read all they could about twins, which was fascinating. She had no idea if her babies were identical or not, or what sex they were and chose not to know. She bought a very modern, efficient twin buggy for the car, but went overboard and ordered a traditional big twin pram as well, as she loved the look of them and the comfort. She began to tire now, as she put on weight and her babies moved a lot and kept her awake, but she stayed well and the midwives were very pleased with her progress.

In mid-October, she was told she might carry full term, as the babies were not too big, although she felt like an elephant. Jenny was wonderful. She ran baths for her and brought ginger biscuits and tea in the mornings and fetched and carried. Between them they decided on a lemon shade for the nursery, with lots of animals on the walls and cosy green carpets on the floor. All was ready.

Her mother began to ring her her regularly over the weeks and was caring and composed. Charles had done his work!

Ella now had backache and was counting the days. Then she had a gripping pain and her lower back one evening in late October, followed by another.

After they both had a brief panic, Jenny rang the hospital and they said Ella was to come in within the next hour or two. The bag was ready and so were they. She had chosen Jenny as her birth partner and she certainly needed her strong hands and calm ways. It was not as bad as she had feared, although, at times, the pain was almost more than she could bear, but it seemed to ease just as she felt she couldn't cope. Jenny scarcely left her side and was a great comfort.

Then, as the late October sun broke through, Ella was working harder than she ever thought she could and suddenly she felt her baby's head emerge.

"Rest now a moment," said the midwife. "Now one long push," and a baby's wavering cry filled the air.

"You have a daughter, Ella," and in her arms was a tiny, red-faced baby, wrapped in towel. She couldn't believe it and before she could, the baby was whisked away while she laboured again.

Laughter and applause shook her out of her pain.

"And a son," somebody cried.

Suddenly, she had a baby in each arm and she bust into tears of joy, as did Jenny.

"You've done it, Ella," the nurse said.

"Really well done. Two 5 pounders and perfect."

It all became a whirlwind after that, but then she was suddenly in a side ward, with a cot either side of the bed and Jenny holding a mug of tea and a round of toast.

"Oh, Ella, they're so perfect and so little, but they said they were big for twins. Drink this tea and we can hold them, the nurse said."

As they were placed in her arms again her happy tears dropped on the tiny scrunched-up faces. A boy and a girl, who were they like?

"They're like nobody at the moment," Jenny laughed, and the nurse said, "Give them a few days to discover who they are," and they all laughed.

Bethan came hot foot at afternoon visiting – she had pulled strings.

"Oh my God, how wonderful," she cried and gave Ella a long hug and a tissue wrapped parcel.

When she unwrapped it she found two exquisite hand made shawls – so fine they were like gossamer.

"Oh, Bethan, they're so beautiful. They must have taken you ages."

"Yes, they did. I began as soon as I knew you were expecting twins. I've had to hide them once or twice when you called. My Nana taught me to crochet when I was a young girl."

"I will treasure them for ever," Ella said as she clasped her friend's hand. "I feel so blessed. The babies are really well and I just have to stay a few days and we'll be home."

All three inspected the little ones. Their eyes were shut tight, their skin was red and they both had black hair stuck to their tiny heads.

"You can't tell if they look the same," Jenny said. "But they can't be identical, can they?"

All agreed that wasn't possible.

"Have you any names ready?" asked Bethan, and Ella said, "I have a little list. I wanted to wait until I saw them first. I have decided to give them one name to let them fit in here, where they will live, and a second to honour Sam's family background." As she spoke his name she began to suddenly cry, big sobs that wretched her tired body. Bethan put the babies back in their cots and made Ella lie down and eat, stroking her hair.

"You cry, love," she said, "but no too much. Have a sleep now and you'll feel better. We'll still be here watching them."

Almost as she spoke Ella drifted off and when she woke her pals were seated either side of the bed. The nurse came in and began to introduce her to breast feeding and the hours flew by. In an old-fashioned gesture, her babies were kept in the nursery overnight and, in the early morning had already changed. They were no longer red and, once or twice, a pair of little eyes would open. She was fascinated by them and more in love than she would have thought possible.

"Hugh Samuel and Gwendoline Amber – welcome to the world." She practised saying the names and they seemed right – Hugh and Gwen – the babies she and Sam had made. *I hope you can see them, my love*, she thought, but she wasn't sad. She was fortunate – how could she be sad and she was never going to make these babies ever feel anything other than love and happiness.

Within days they were home – all three and ensconced in their cosy home. She had been told the fresh air was good for them and to only keep them in when it was foggy or bitter, so, even though it was early November, the big pram was delivered and they were wrapped in their shawls and paraded down the hill and into the village. Early days as they were Ella felt full of life and couldn't wait to show off her babies. The trippers had all gone and the locals made a great fuss of them all. Twins were quite a rarity in the village and people had grown to like this tall, elegant English girl. She and Jenny struggled through the nights and she had to learn how to adapt her body to feeding two babies at the same time, which sometimes happened. At least she got more of a break between feeds that way. Jenny was incredible. She bounded upstairs at the first cry and brought the babies to Ella and she did all the housework and cooking in those first weeks. Ella realized she could not have done it all without her. As it was, it was very hard work, but it was happy work and Hugh and Gwen became people in their own right.

Chapter 39

Annie and Charles would come on a flying visit – just one night at Tudor's place and flying into Manchester.

They came when the babies were three weeks old and were instantly besotted by them. They brought with them a whole bag of very chic baby clothes, some of them tiny and some for later.

"When were you thinking of having them christened?" Annie asked "We'd like to be here for that."

The question quite threw Ella, who hadn't given it a moment's thought and she was vague about it.

"Well, let us know as soon as you're decided," said ma. She and Jenny talked about it, when they were on their own again. Sam's sister had already asked whether it would be possible to bring Sam's parents to see their grandchildren in the spring. She and Rav planned to drive them up as Sam's mother would not be able to face the long train trip. All these factors made Ella realize that she did want her babies to have a baptism ceremony – but where?

She had attended Mass a few times at the small church in the village, but she didn't know the priest, who seemed to cover a few parishes. She wasn't sure she wanted to christen them as Catholics anyway. After all, Sam had been a person who didn't seem to need, or want, any religion in his life. What should she do? She and Jenny talked about it a great deal in the run up to a very quiet Christmas – just the four of them, but with quite a lot of callers.

First up was the local choir, come especially up the lane to greet two new little lives. That was an emotional visit. Bethan came on Christmas Eve with gifts for them all and Tudor informed them that he was delivering their Christmas meal. People were so generous. To cap it all, a knock on the door late on Christmas Eve brought a reluctant young Dai. He had carved two exquisite Welsh spoons – one for a baby boy and one for a baby girl. Ella was so delighted that she gave him a big hug. They were so lovely that she hung them, as soon as she could, on the wall of the living room.

She and Jenny had bought the babies silver rattles, which seemed enough, as they had no idea that they were having their first Christmas. However, they were starting to look around, and the candles attracted their notice. *Probably my last time with candles for a long while*, Ella thought.

Hugh and Gwen were putting on weight satisfactorily and Ella still coped with feeding them. Gwen still had her mop of black hair, but Hugh's was wearing thin in patches and, under it, was a golden down. They both had brown eyes and Gwen's skin was a very light coffee colour. They were not going to be all that alike. Ella knew that they would be no more like each other than any other siblings. She told Sam's father one evening, when he made one of his regular phone calls.

"They will be their own person," he said. "Not a copy of any other. How I long to see them. Would March perhaps be alright?"

He was always so courteous and she knew how much all this must mean to a man like him.

She answered him by telling him she was about to make arrangements for a baptism and realized she was now committed.

Then Tudor came up with a brilliant suggestion.

"If the room at Glen-y-Widdw is licensed for weddings, why not have a ceremony there? The young chap at that church is very modern. He comes in for a meal sometimes. Shall I introduce you to him?"

Within a week they had a call and then a visit. He was ordained in the Church of Wales but had no problem with the idea of an 'open' baptism, in the circumstances.

"The important thing is to register these little souls with the good Lord, so that He can look out for them," he laughed. Suddenly it was sorted and a Sunday in March was chosen. The vicar took responsibility for booking the room and Ella arranged for afternoon tea to be served in the conservatory.

Netta called her and asked her, "Would you mind very much if my parents brought the outfits Sam and I were blessed in? It would mean so much to them."

"No, not at all," Ella answered. Her babies seemed to be making a lot of people happy.

Gaynor took over then. She printed tasteful invitations and

promised to put some flowers about the place and she asked about godparents, as the vicar had said that, of course, there should be godparents, as many as you like as long as your son has to men and your daughter two women. In the end, there were quite a bunch of them. Joel and Tudor and Netta stood for Hugh and Bethan and Jenny and Rav for Gwen.

All the guests stayed at Tudor's hotel and they made a great mix of ages and colours and nationalities. Lots of photos were taken and there was lots of laughter and joy.

Sam's father had brought with him a phial of holy oil and he had quietly asked the vicar for permission to bless his grandchildren and that was very moving. All in all, it was a very joyous few days.

Chapter 40

And then it all returned to normal. Ella and Jenny had a little pattern to their days. The babies were, mostly, very easy. They had unsettled days and nights, as all little ones do, but they were healthy and thriving. They began to settle into a happy little rhythm and they all went to baby swim class, near Nefyn, once a week. The twins were now weaned onto bottles and Ella had more free time. She used it to wander the fields, collecting wool from gates and walls to add to the bag she had begun.

Jenny worked behind the bar 2 or 3 nights a week, once the babies were settled. They had outgrown the cradles and were in the other bedroom. There were two cots, next to each other, as they liked being close.

One of the best bits of the day was early evening, when they undressed them and lay them on a blanket, by the fire, for a naked romp. They were so happy being close and it was such fun to watch them.

Ella found a wooden playpen and put them in there to roll around. She was so very content. When they were settled the two girls had their meal and relaxed for a few hours. Ella had begun to card her wool and Bethan had offered to give her spinning lessons. Young Dai and Jenny had a drink or a walk sometimes, all very casual.

Once Hugh and Gwen were sturdy enough to use the pushchair they spent a lot of time on the beach. The harbour beach was easily accessible and there were little rocky coves, in which to shelter from sun or breeze and life was pretty good.

Ella thought often about Sam and longed for him to share her life and see his babies. She only had a few photos of him. But she had one enlarged and had a copy on the nursery wall, as she was determined her babies would know who their father was. She had her sad times, but two healthy little souls kept her busy.

Almost before she knew it, the first birthday was near. Hugh was crawling and into mischief by then and Gwen just sat on the floor and watched him. The two girls gave a lot of thought and decided that a wooden truck, filled with wooden bricks would encourage Hugh to start to walk. For quiet, dreamy Gwen they found a cradle and baby doll, and a few friends came for tea. They didn't, as yet, know any other children, but in the New Year they started going to Toddler Club, where they all met new people.

They were all part of Abersoch now, and made welcome everywhere. As there was a constant battle to keep up numbers for the village school, the twins were going to be a bonus.

Ella did an odd day at the lifeboat shop and picked up the spinning very well – so well that Bethan lent her spinning wheel on extended loan and she began to produce and dye small quantities of wool and using them to do small cushions and the like. The craft shop was more than happy to sell them on for her and she felt fulfilled to be using her skills.

Then she had an upsetting call from Sam's sister. Her mother had slipped away, in her sleep. Netta was very upset and her father inconsolable. They were such a loving couple. Ella shed some tears herself and then rang Netta back to ask about funeral arrangements. She was told, very definitely that she was not to make such a trip and it would, in accordance with their tradition, be very soon. Most Sundays Ella went to Mass and lit some candles and prayed for the old lady's soul. She wrote to Mr Patel and, some weeks later, a parcel arrived with a reply. He had sent her some beautiful silk saris, as he knew of her love of fabric. She was so touched and she put them away to decide how to use them.

It was a long, wet, stormy winter, but suddenly the days became longer and the early flowers peeped out. Even though this was her home now she couldn't believe how long she had lived here and she had more days when she didn't think of Sam. Time had begun its healing. Also, she was occupied with her lovely toddlers and her weaving, as well as running a home. Sam would never be far away, but the memories grew into more pleasant, loving ones, rather than awful grief.

One morning, as the four of them were in the village with hot chocolate, outside the Deli, the saw a poster at the end of a narrow and private lane, so they walked up to read it. It announced that Mr and Mrs Parry-Jones would invite all to a Hog Roast on a Saturday in

May. There would be live music, a bar and stalls. All proceeds to the Hospice on the Llyn and the RNLI. It sounded interesting.

Later they queried Bethan about it. She told them that the Parry-Joneses lived in the big house, on the cliff overlooking the yacht club beach and that they were very nice people. Then she said, "Why don't you two young things go while I babysit? You never have a night out." So it was settled.

Ella made a long skirt from one of the saris and had a T-shirt to pick out a colour. The weather was often glorious in May, but she had a homemade shawl just in case. With Bethan in charge they strolled into the village centre and followed other people up the lane. It was all very festive, with bunting and lights in the trees. There was a fair-sized house, on the left of the lane and ahead of them, a substantial Victorian building, There was a marquee to the side and it was already busy, with jolly people of all ages. A jazz band played at one side of the lawn and there was a glorious smell of food.

Jenny knew more people than Ella and she had gone for the jeans and boots option. There was a wide range of dress, so they both fitted in. They joined a small group in the bar tent and chatted to them for a while. Ella was fascinated by this place and wondered if it faced a beach. Everywhere around her twisted and turned so much that she was never sure which way she was facing. After a while she told Jenny she was going for an explore and they arranged to meet up for food. There were a few other folk exploring, so she wandered off around a path at the side of the house and, suddenly, she was near a cliff top with the beach huts below and a glorious view, from a different angle. It was quite breathtaking and she found a flat rock to perch on and take it all in. She sat for quite a time. She liked her own company and could hear plenty of laughter and noise behind her.

Somebody spoke into a mike and there began the sounds of a guitar being tuned and applause from the crowd.

Then a piece of music she knew so well, but never listened to and a man's melodious voice drifting over the shrubs. He was singing 'Alleluia' and Ella's heart missed a beat. As the music continued she began to weep. She cried for herself and for her children, who would never have a daddy, and she cried for Sam, her brave, wonderful Sam. The floodgates really burst and she sat there sobbing.

Minutes must have gone by and she realized there was somebody close by. She lifted her face and a man was walking towards her. She rubbed at her eyes. It was the vet.

"Are you OK? You don't seem to be," and he sat on the rock. "Can you tell me why you're so upset, not being nosy, but I don't like to see you like this. Can I fetch your partner?"

Ella sniffed. "I haven't got a partner, which is why I am upset. 'Alleluia' was his favourite song and when I heard it being sung so well, it just set me off."

He pulled her shawl up around her shoulders.

"Sorry if I put my foot in it, it was me singing and I see you around with your twins and with a big bloke pushing the pram – I assumed!"

"Oh, that is Joel, an old and good friend." She hesitated and then it all came pouring out – Sam and then her twins – her reasons for moving here – she told him it all.

When she had finished there was a long silence.

"I think we could both do with a drink," as he helped her to her feet. He put his hand under her elbow and they went back to join the rest.

Later, sitting on a bench with Jenny, eating supper, she was quizzed. Why had she been crying? What had the vet to do with it, and so she explained.

"I felt quite teary myself," Jenny said.

Much later, as they sat over a nightcap, with Bethan, at the cottage they spoke of the house in its lovely setting. She told them that the Parry-Joneses were a branch of the family who had once owned Glen-y-Wyddw and most of the peninsula. Mr Parry-Jones is a well-known architect and their son is the young vet. A nice family – no side to them.

Mid-morning the day later a van pulled up and a girl came down the path with a really glorious display of spring blooms, in a basket. The card said 'For a very brave young lady' and she knew where they came from.

Jenny was even more thrilled than she was and it lifted the whole day.

"I don't even know his name."

"Obviously his surname is Parry-Jones and I am pretty sure he is Gareth. I'll check in the bar."

True to her word she asked some questions. His name was Gareth and he was the son of the Parry-Joneses, who lived in the big house. They were in some way related to the family who used to live at Glen-y-Wyddw. Gareth lived in the house on the same little lane. He was about 32 or so.

"Stop, stop," Jenny laughed. "Have you got his DNA?" at which they both laughed and carried on with hanging out the washing.

Chapter 41

The next time they came cross each other in the village he crossed over to chat.

"Fancy a coffee?" he asked them both.

Jenny decided she would carry on with the shopping and he and Ella sat out in a watery sun.

"I'm Gareth," he said, "and you must he Ella," he smiled.

He played about with the twins and they laughed at his antics.

"They are a lovely pair," he said, "and so unalike. Are they always this happy?"

"Mostly they are. They enjoy each others' company, which helps a lot."

Jenny came back and Gareth went off towards his home. Then he turned back.

"Jenny, would you babysit if Ella and I had a drink one night?"

She grinned at them both.

"Of course I will, but not on a Saturday. Tudor is always busy then."

So they sorted it there and then.

He picked her up in his Discovery and they went to a small pub somewhere in the wilds and away from gossip and they talked and talked and talked.

And so it began.

Chapter 42

Ella had never imagined she could fall in love again, but, almost before she realized it, it was happening.

He was gentle and thoughtful – more extroverted than Sam and he and the children got on famously. Ella was wary at first, terrified of being hurt, but slowly her barriers were being turned over.

It was a while before he really kissed her, more than a peck on the cheek, but when he did she found herself melting into his big arms and wanting it never to stop. Jenny was so excited and had to contain her joy at this turn of events. She was growing very close to young Dai and they talked and giggled together, as girls do when they are falling in love.

The season began and the village filled up. A young farmer's wife, out on the Nefyn road had twin boys and Bethan brought her to see Ella for some tips. She really felt part of the village now and so did Jenny.

It was a very hit and miss Summer – a lot of showers and not much hot sun. Ella found time now to do some weaving, while the twins played around the house. Gwen was the leader and Hugh pottered about in her wake. They were bright, or so Ella thought, and she was teaching them colours etc. They were good mixers at Toddler Club, but were always looking out for each other. Gareth was a regular caller at the cottage and he asked them all to lunch at his house one weekend. It was a sturdy stone house, facing the bay with old steps cut out of the rock, leading to an ancient boathouse. There were two big living rooms and four bedrooms and it was comfy, if not rather masculine. He was given it by his parents for his 21st and knew how lucky he was. He did pasta for them all – a big favourite of Hugh and Gwen's and dragged a few of his old wooden toys out of a cupboard. They had a lovely afternoon.

He worked long hours at the surgery and was 'on call' for the lifeboat as well, but they managed to see each other a couple of times a week.

Gradually, they got to know each others back stories and to really know and understand each other and slowly they fell in love.

The months went by very pleasantly. Ella started the twins at nursery for just one afternoon a week. It was hard to leave them at first, but they really took to it and would ask every day if it was today – their school.

Summer slid into Autumn – one to make up for Summer and then a bonfire on the beach and fireworks. Winter brought a couple of deaths in the village and the odd bits of gossip and scandal and they battened down hatches for a very cold winter.

Chapter 43

Now, suddenly, a whole year had passed, since the evening of the Hog Roast.

Ella sat on a flat rock, just above the ebbing tide while her children drew lines in the damp sand. A tall, raven-haired, man came striding down the stone steps, holding ice cream cornets in his big hands.

"Dada, Dada," cried the children as they ran to him and wrapped around his bare legs.

"Steady now," he laughed as he sat on the rock by Ella and handed out the ices.

"So, how is Mrs Parry-Jones today?"

"Very happy and very well, thank you, sir."

She took his hand and placed it on her stomach.

"Hold still," she told him, "and you will feel our baby kick," and so they were – this little tableau and, in the sound of the ripping waves, somewhere far away she heard Sam's voice.

"Carpe Diem, Ella, Carpe Diem."

20087239R00095

Printed in Great Britain
by Amazon